MARINARA

By Mr. & Mrs. Post

ISBN 979-8-218-30023-4

First edition 2023
Copper Bell Press
Cover Art by Peabody

Visit us at marinarabook.com

For Fizzo

Authors' Note

This book is similar to a garment tag that says, "this is a one-of-a-kind item, and any anomalies are part of the unique dyeing process." In other words, it is presented exactly as intended. There is purpose behind every grammatical and structural choice. These artistic liberties are not overwhelming but should be noted so as not to be confused with carelessness. Furthermore, this book is untouched by the hands of outside influences. The relationship from author to reader could not possibly be any more intimate. Directly from our hearts to your eyes, just as we intended. Now buckle up. As Ben will say later on, "Are you ready?"

-Mr. & Mrs. Post

MARINARA

CHAPTER ONE

"You wanna hear a story, kid?"

Ben whipped around to face the door, startled by the sudden voice in the room. "I was just... looking... for..." he stuttered, trying desperately to come up with something, anything that explained why he was snooping around the papers on The Janitor's desk.

"Gimme that," The Janitor said as he took a faded folder from Ben's hand. He motioned to a rickety stool in the corner of the room. "Sit down."

Ben approached the stool cautiously, one eye on The Janitor as he tried to read the man's expression and gauge whether he was about to get a real tongue-lashing.

You didn't wanna mess with the guy. He had been at Marinara cleaning up the disgusting messes of over-hyped children in pizza and video game frenzies since the beginning of time, and he had the disposition to prove it. His face was weathered beyond his years, his brow constantly furrowed, and his thin frame clearly had a lot of miles on the engine. He had the rough, gravelly voice of a lifelong smoker, but Ben had never seen him light up. He had, however, seen him take to the bottle on many an occasion. It seemed like he had a fifth of Jack glued to the palm of his hand.

The Janitor did not subscribe to the social norms of sharing his name with his coworkers. Instead, whenever he met a new employee, he simply referred to himself as The Janitor. Ben almost relished watching new recruits meet the guy, not knowing how to respond when they saw first-hand how guarded he was.

The Janitor held up the folder he had taken from Ben. "You wanna know what this is?" he said. Ben froze, not sure if there was a right answer to the question. He did want to know though. He'd barely gotten a chance to look at those peculiar old news clippings he'd stumbled upon inside of it before he got caught.

The Janitor opened the folder, then seemed to drift to a faraway place. "My father was a decent man," he began.

Ben breathed a silent sigh of relief. *I guess it's just story time. Maybe he thought I was looking for next week's schedule or something.*

"He was a prison guard at the old state pen right outside of town. He worked on D-block, but everyone called it The Dark. It was where they kept the worst of the worst—child killers, rapists… evil, evil men."

The Janitor looked down at the floor, avoiding Ben's attentive gaze. "It was a living."

After a few dry coughs he continued on. "We had a workshop in our basement, and the two of us were always down there tinkering or building something when he wasn't at work. Those were good days. Then the job started to take its toll on my father. The joy and life just seemed to seep out of him as

10

the years wore on. Over time he stopped tossing the football and started tossing back the bottle. I know it wasn't easy on him, but I couldn't help but look at him as weak."

Ben started to fidget a little on the stool. The Janitor's office was windowless and stuffy, and two people in there were more than enough to make anyone feel claustrophobic. He wasn't sure why The Janitor was telling him all this. All he knew was he had better damn well pay attention because he didn't want to do anything to jeopardize the deal they'd made earlier. It was what he'd come in there to talk about in the first place before curiosity got the better of him. Ben needed that key. He was going to throw the greatest graduation party of all time.

Ben wasn't usually a party type of kid. He was more of a stay at home to get ahead on his homework and play board games with his little sister on the weekend type of kid, while all the cool teenagers ran around town raising hell. But at the start of senior year he'd gotten an after-school job at Marinara. Free pizza, soda and video games weren't the worst way to make a buck and meet new friends. They were nice perks, but this party would be worth every ounce of bullshit he'd ever had to put up with at work. Ben knew if he could pull this off, he'd have done something big, really big. Maybe even big enough to impress the girl of his dreams, Sarah.

"Hey kid, you still listenin'?" The Janitor barked, snapping his fingers at Ben's face.

Ben snapped out of it. "Yeah… yes, I'm definitely listening," he said, trying to sound as interested as possible.

The Janitor looked hard at Ben for a moment, his eyes squinting with doubt, then proceeded. "It's funny the mundane things you remember when those things are linked with

11

something tragic. We had meatloaf and peas that night, eating dinner together at the kitchen table like we usually did before my father would leave for the night shift. I still remember him pushing meat around on his plate, not really eating anything. He wouldn't meet our eyes, not even my mother's. After a while, he slowly pushed his chair back from the table and stood up. 'Thank you for a lovely meal,' he said. There was no emotion. He wore no expression. He didn't say goodbye or kiss my mother on the forehead like he always did. He just walked straight out the front door, and all we heard was that old Buick start up and rumble off into the distance. Dad went to work that night, and he never came home."

The Janitor finally took a pause as his eyes drifted back to that faraway place. "Some of the worst things are done with the best intentions," he whispered, so quietly it was as if the thought was only meant for him.

"My mother loved old quotes. She had a book full of them, and I'd flip through it every now and again. One of them always stuck with me: 'All concerns of men go wrong when they wish to cure evil with evil.'"

The Janitor picked up a box cutter sitting on his desk and slid out the blade. His thumb flicked back and forth on the thin, sharp steel.

"That night a massive fire broke out at the prison. It started after lights out when the inmates were locked in their cells sleeping. There was only one guard on duty, and it was my father. The entire D-block burned to the ground. Poor bastards didn't have a chance. Every one of them burned alive in their metal cages. They say you could hear the screams from miles away. By the time it was out, most of the bodies were so badly charred that they couldn't even identify which prisoner was which. Just a pile of scorched black death and bones.

"The police chalked it up to faulty wiring in the old building. No one back then would ever question an officer, and in all honesty I'm not sure anyone really cared that much about a bunch of dead criminals. But I had my suspicions. I worked up the nerve and asked him only one time. He looked me right in the eye and calmly said, 'We all have to die.' That was it and that was the last time we ever spoke of it."

Oh my gosh, Ben thought. *That fire. That's what the top article was about in the folder.* The great prison fire was practically town lore by now. Every kid knew, or at least thought they knew, all about it. Ben wasn't sure what he should say or if he should even say anything at all. But now he was wholly intrigued. He just wanted to ask The Janitor why he was telling all this to him.

"Lock the door," The Janitor instructed Ben. He always mysteriously locked the door whenever he was in his office. The jokes made around Marinara about what he was doing in there were what one might expect. Nevertheless, it was slightly strange behavior.

The Janitor grabbed a bottle of Jack Daniels from inside a drawer and took a three count of what one might call a swig. He reached the bottle out towards Ben. "Want a hit?"

Ben thought for an excuse fast and hard. So fast and hard that he didn't come up with anything at all. "Sure," he said, pressing it against his lips and tilting it high enough and long enough that it looked like he drank much more than he actually did. And even though he tried his absolute best to avoid it, the punishing bitterness of charcoal and leather made him wince the sourest of winces. Ben handed the bottle back to The

Janitor, who promptly picked up where he left off with both the whiskey and his words.

"My father was never the same again after that night. He struggled with having done what he believed needed to be done, while living with the guilt of the unpunished crime he had committed. That was his life sentence. He never went back to work, but it wasn't long before he began going back to the prison. He would drive out to the blackened debris day after day, salvaging metal beams, old grey bricks or whatever he could take that might be reusable. He then spent every waking moment building with his bare hands the structure you're standing in now."

This was the prison? Ben wasn't easily spooked, but he felt a light chill run down his spine. The kind he would feel during a campfire ghost story told deep in the woods on a cold, black night back in Boy Scouts.

"My father vowed to spend the rest of his life creating a place where he could bring joy to others. He started off building a penny arcade in the late-fifties, but by the time it was finished, those were a thing of the past. When it was finally complete almost a quarter century later, it opened as a video arcade. The day of the grand opening my father walked into the woods right behind here, and we never saw him again. That was over five years ago. So I took this post to make sure his life's work was always watched over and never neglected."

"I'm sorry about your dad," Ben said, and he meant it. Ben had a great dad. He was the kind of all-American dad you saw in a Sizzler commercial hoisting his son on his shoulders after a little league game. It made him sad to imagine the kind of childhood The Janitor must have had with a father like that.

"Don't be sorry kid, and don't be stupid either," The Janitor replied.

"Okay," Ben said, slightly offended. "I better get back to work now."

The Janitor nodded and unlocked the door but not before a parting message. "And next time ask before you go rummaging around my shit."

Once he was back out on the gaming floor Ben felt like a weight had been lifted. He took a deep breath of popcorn-laced air and began to focus on what he had left to do so he could get out of there early. He'd have to get the key tomorrow because he sure as hell wasn't going to strike up another conversation with The Janitor tonight.

Ben looked over the gaming floor and spotted a familiar face. There was a little kid who came to the arcade almost every day after school. He was always by himself, always dressed in raggedy hand-me-down clothes, and he always seemed a little bit sad. He never played any games but would watch other kids play with a glimmer in his eye. Ben wasn't sure what the kid was trying to get away from, but he made sure to let him know he was there if he wanted to talk. The kid never wanted to talk though. He just wanted to escape for a while.

Ben did a quick scan of the room to see where hard-ass shift manager Darcy was. When he spotted her tied up with the Frogger arcade trying to help a frantic kid get a stuck token out, he made a beeline for the prize counter where the register was. He wasn't supposed to "abuse his position" by giving tokens to his "freeloader friends" as shift manager Darcy relished telling him. But Ben believed that sometimes it was okay to commit a small wrong in order to do something good.

Ben reached into the token bin and pulled out a handful. He walked back over to the little kid who was now watching a group of kids in the dining pit having a He-Man themed birthday party. Ben tapped the kid on the shoulder, as he had done several times before, and opened the palm of his hand. The kid's eyes always lit up like Christmas morning when he saw the token bounty. "These are for you. Go have some fun," Ben said. The kid slowly extended his cupped hands, like a cautious dog taking a treat from a stranger.

"Thank you," he said gratefully.

"You're welcome," Ben said, as he smiled both inside and out. The smile was almost as big, but not quite as stupid, as the one he'd given Sarah when she waved at him between second and third period that morning.

The rest of his shift passed quickly, and by 8 o'clock Ben was exhausted. The kids had been especially rowdy tonight. One of the boys from the He-Man birthday party had been charging around the arcade shouting, "I have the power!" and whacking unsuspecting gamers with his plastic sword all night. When the parents decided to do nothing about it, the job fell to Ben to rein him in.

He usually stayed after work to beat his own high scores on some of the arcades, but tonight he needed to get home so he could pick out the perfect outfit, work on some one-liners and reluctantly get a full body workout if time permitted. Not to mention try to get a good night's sleep with all the anticipation. It was a very big day tomorrow.

PRISON BURNS!

BY JIM RICHARDS

Late last evening an entire wing of the state penitentiary located just outside of town burned to the ground. The section destroyed was known for housing the state's most demented and sadistic offenders. It was operating at full capacity at the time the fire broke out, and as attested by a medical examiner at the scene, there were no survivors. Police have been quick to dismiss the idea of foul play, although a formal investigation is still forthcoming.

The incinerated wing was of particular notoriety, so much so that it carried a nickname. Although officials referred to it as the D-Block, it was known amongst prisoners as "The Dark."

There are multiple rumored origins of the bestowed handle. One of which is that lights went out uncommonly early in order to quell the excessive violence. Another is the controversial use of what's considered by many an archaic form of punishment. That is the practice of throwing prisoners in "the hole," a brutal form of solitary confinement. Lastly, and perhaps most chilling, is the suspiciously high amount of suicides, particularly hangings, amongst the prisoners in the wing.

One of the few former inmates lucky enough to be released, Matthew Wayne Snyder, had this to say about his time in The Dark: "I can't tell you the things that went on in there. You wouldn't understand." He had no further comments.

The unknown cause of the fire didn't seem to be of much concern to witnesses of the event but was rather a means to an end. Local phone operator Becky Maye had pulled over on the side of the road as she and her husband watched the flames rise. "I think it's fitting the devils burned in the fire," she said. Her remarks echoed the general feeling of those interviewed. Asked if she had any sympathy for the men burned alive: "Zero," she replied. The only hint of concern expressed by more than a few bystanders was a fear of taxes raising in order to fund construction for a new wing.

Continued on Page 7

CHAPTER TWO

The halls of Reagan High flooded with students eager to get the weekend started as the final bell rang. Emily Stuart was one of Reagan's top students, but she was pretty enough and cool enough to have earned a place in the upper echelon of high school society rather than a spot at the mathletes' lunch table.

Emily pulled a few books out of her locker and started to zip up her backpack when her friend Chrissy Walker saddled up next to her. "Hey girl! Mind if I borrow some mousse?" Chrissy said, already pulling a can of L'Oréal from Emily's locker.

Chrissy was Reagan's resident "it girl," and she was every bit as blonde and pink and bubble gum chewing as one might imagine. "Were you able to get the night off tonight?" she asked, staring into Emily's locker mirror as she meticulously worked in the foam hold.

"Noooo," Emily said, drawing out the word to emphasize her disappointment. "They couldn't give it to me. We're still understaffed."

"Still? Who wouldn't want to work at an animal shelter with all those little cuties?" Chrissy asked.

"Me. On a Friday night," Emily sassed. "But if you're that interested, I could probably get you a job."

"Oh, I'm good thanks," Chrissy said. "I don't do well with things that pee and poop and vomit and shed. Just get there as soon as you can. You know how the boys get."

Emily did know exactly how the boys got. Really drunk. Really fast. Down for the count by midnight half the time. "Brad's gonna be passed out by the time I get there," she said, only partially joking.

"Oh for sure," Chrissy scoffed. "After he pees or throws up on something of course. I'm sorry Emily, I just don't know what you see in him."

"You should give him a chance," Emily said. "He's really sweet when you get to—"

Just then, as if on cue, Brad Reynolds came tearing around the corner at full speed, chasing down a football in mid-air. Coach had done a fine job with Brad. Not only was he all-state, but he always kept his eye on the ball, even at his own expense—or the expense of anyone around him. Brad snagged the ball over the outstretched hands of his imaginary opponent and clobbered into a poor kid unlucky enough to be standing where he landed.

"Touchdown!" Brad hopped to his feet and helped the annihilated bystander up. Although he was rambunctious, he was the kind of guy that would give you the shirt off his back. "Sorry man. That one got away from us," Brad said, his letterman's jacket announcing who he was so he didn't have to. He tucked the ball under his arm, then meandered over to Emily.

"Hey babe," he said as he threw his other arm around her shoulder. Emily tilted her cheek towards Brad and popped her index finger against it in the universal language for gimme some sugar. Instead of complying, Brad did the exact same thing against his cheek, and so they just stood there playing a sick game of chicken while Chrissy stared blankly at them. Emily begrudgingly gave in, knowing full well Brad would take it into the next hour if dared to. After all that was squared away, he finally got around to acknowledging Chrissy.

"Oh, hi Brad," Chrissy said sarcastically, brushing off the front of her designer clothes as if his mere presence had dirtied them somehow. Brad gave Chrissy an exaggerated smirk, then turned back to Emily.

He leaned into her ear with a moderately seductive whisper. "I am so pumped for tonight."

"They're having me close again," Emily said with a hesitancy that indicated she'd told him that line a time or two before.

"Are you freaking serious?!" Brad said, immediately reverting back to rambunctious jock. "They're dogs. They eat their own shit. I think they'll be okay for one night."

Chrissy couldn't hide the disdain on her face as was often the case when she was forced to interact with Brad. Her burden had been endured countless times throughout history whenever a friend was forced to tolerate another friend's significant other. "Don't be a dick Brad," she said.

Brad ignored Chrissy completely as he went back to the well once more for a sugary sweet, almost vomit inducing guilt trip on his girlfriend. "It's just that tonight's a really special night muffin, and it won't be half as special without you there."

"It's special to me too," Emily replied, side-eyeing Chrissy who was pretending to dry heave in the background. "But I still have to go home after work to shower and change. I'll be there at twelve on the dot. I promise."

"Twelve?!" Brad yelled, before restraining himself. "That's perfect, I'll be waiting," he calmly replied.

"Good afternoon ladies," a voice crooned from down the hall as Keaton James appeared in all his glory. Keaton had been blessed with all-American chiseled features, perfectly messy jet-black hair and a twinkle in his eye that made the girls swoon. Whatever charm he possessed though, he also had an equal dose of sarcasm to match.

As he walked up, Keaton's eyes were so magnetically drawn to Chrissy's ass that he was certain the name Jordache would be associated with any perfect ass he'd see for the rest of his life.

He put a hand on Brad's shoulder. "Girls, I've gotta steal Casanova away from you. Try to hold the tears. We've got business to discuss."

Brad gave Emily a peck on the cheek. "Eleven. I'll see you at eleven," he said, and Emily couldn't help but smile as she waved him away.

Keaton gave Chrissy "the eye" as he walked away from the lockers with Brad. "See you tonight," he said.

"See ya," Chrissy replied. She gazed as he walked into the distance, then slammed her locker shut with excitement. "Did you see that look he gave me?" she exclaimed to Emily. "I sure hope he's not expecting any tonight, 'cause I just might have to give it to him," she said, biting her lip.

"Hooker!" Emily said, whacking her friend's arm.

"I know!" Chrissy squealed enthusiastically. She linked her arm through Emily's, and they started off down the hall together.

****

Brad and Keaton walked along a row of parked cars in the school's student lot. It wasn't the kind of town where kids were given shiny, brand new cars on their sixteenth birthday. It was the kind of town where teens got summer jobs to earn enough scratch to buy a car that would have been very nice just ten years earlier. If it wasn't a hand-me-down or found in Auto Trader, it could be haggled for at the local dealership—they were always waiting for some poor high school kids to come and take junkers off their hands.

"Man, midnight? That sucks," Keaton said, sympathizing with his friend.

"No shit," Brad replied. "I was hoping to seal the deal tonight. At least you have all night to work on Chrissy."

"I doubt it takes all night," Keaton said, self-assured as ever. "Did you see that look she gave me?"

"Yeah, I think you melted her panties," Brad said.

Two sophomore girls walking by overheard and shot the boys a dirty look as they passed. Keaton called out to them, "It's not what it sounds like." He then wondered what else *could* that possibly mean, as he now wasn't even sure he understood the original statement.

"Your panties can be next!" Brad playfully yelled at them. The more homely one looked back with a smile. One out of two wasn't bad.

As the guys approached the end of the lot, Keaton stopped. "Where'd you park dude?" he asked.

"*I* didn't park anywhere," Brad replied. "I'm looking for Ben's truck. He hitched a ride to work and gave me ten bucks to wax his chariot for tonight. Seemed like a better deal at the time."

Brad looked around confused, then slowly motioned his index finger like a compass needle until it landed confidently on a direction. Keaton shook his head as he followed Brad back to where they had just walked from.

"You do realize the historical potential of tonight, right?" Keaton asked.

"Yes," Brad replied. "I am looking forward to my first non-hand delivered orgasm." Brad's face contorted into a mask of moronic pleasure, his eyes rolling back in his head and mouth open wide as his tongue slurped out. Just then, by serendipitous chance, the two sophomore girls passed by again, grossed out by the bizarre display of feigned sexual climax. Unfazed, Brad yelled out, "But that's not gonna happen if Ben doesn't get that key!"

"We got the biggest damn bottle of Jack in town. He'll get it," Keaton said.

"Lemme see," Brad said.

The boys stopped walking and Keaton swung his backpack around and unzipped it. He shot a covert look around the parking lot to make sure they weren't being watched, then halfway pulled out a massive handle of whiskey. It was more than twice as big as a regular sized bottle one might see at a store or in their parents' "secret" cabinet.

"That's the most beautiful thing I've ever seen," Brad said, admiring the honey colored nectar that was going to barter their way into unsupervised self-destruction. "May I?" he asked, reaching out to touch it. Keaton immediately zipped up the bag.

"I've been lugging this damn thing around all day. Now I gotta go drop it off to Ben at Marinara because he was too big of a wiener to take it on school grounds. Thank God we don't have liquor sniffing dogs on campus," Keaton joked.

"If we did, I'd pour tequila all over my balls," Brad replied.

"You're a weird dude," Keaton said as the two continued their journey to find Ben's truck. "And speaking of weird dudes, if that creepy old janitor doesn't take our peace offering tonight, he's either A, crazier than I thought or B, not nearly the alcoholic we all gave him credit for."

"I wish Ben could've gotten a job at Showbiz," Brad said. "Marinara kind of blows."

"If Ben had a job at corporate shithole Showbiz, we wouldn't even be having this talk," Keaton countered. "Besides, Marinara has that funky, run-down charm you can only get from an indie."

One of them finally spotted Ben's truck, and Brad pulled out a set of keys. "True. On a side note, if Ben pulls this off, there's a ninety-nine percent chance I take a shit in the ball pit tonight."

"My God, man," Keaton said.

Brad unlocked the driver's side door and slid into Ben's pride and joy—a blue Chevy short-bed pickup. Ben was damn proud of that handsome, old truck. He had worked too hard and long not to be.

Brad turned the engine over a few times before revving it up. He reached his arm down and spun his fist in a circular motion to manually roll down the window.

As the truck peeled out of the parking lot, an angry teacher came running out of the building. "That's detention Ben Cooper!"

Brad yelled back to Keaton. "See ya tonight bud!

CHAPTER THREE

Marinara was quite literally in the middle of nowhere. Long country roads, some of them dirt, were its only connections to town. Nobody ever just happened upon the place. You were either headed to it or passing by it.

The facade was bland and unwelcoming, a brick and mortar stamp of humankind's infringement on nature. The woods behind it were, like most woods, a bit eerie and mysterious, yet even they felt lively and maybe even inviting in contrast to the dull exterior of Marinara. The front of the building had only a single glass door in the center, while the rest of the structure was completely devoid of windows. It's resemblance to a seedy gentlemen's club had caused it to be mistaken for one more than a time or two. In contrast to everything else though, the signage in all capitals was eye-catching. Big, bold, neon red letters lent a hint that there might be something more to the place.

Inside was a much less depressing version of itself, albeit still worn and rough around the edges. Custom built from the ground up, it curiously contained an inordinate amount of rooms—like rooms on top of rooms. The carpets were a dark collage of spilt sodas, painted over the many years. The walls consisted of muted browns and yellows and probably could have used a fresh coat years ago. But there was a reason why people came from near and far. It was the glowing screens and flashing lights of every arcade and interactive game imaginable that were hypnotic to both children and teens alike. 8-bit beeps and pops composed simple melodies that became one exhilarating hodgepodge of sound. Children's euphoric laughs, screams and squeals were the only proof one needed to know it was indeed a kid's paradise.

Ben had gotten to Marinara as soon as he could to start his shift for the night. This was his last chance to get the key from The Janitor, and he wasn't going to blow it. Ben's friend Perry Blackwell had been happy to give him a ride. He'd planned on dropping by anyway, as he often did whenever he was looking for an excuse to avoid his homework or chores and play free video games instead.

Perry was a stoner. When it came to weed there were two kinds of guys—those who smoked occasionally at a party with friends and those who did that and then the next day smoked by themselves in their basement. Perry was the latter.

He and Ben had bonded over their love of Godzilla movies back in the sixth grade. They'd made a routine out of getting together on Friday nights to watch them on VHS tapes rented from Blockbuster. Towards the later years, Perry was always high during their marathons; but Ben didn't take a single toke—he never needed an excuse to watch a Godzilla movie.

Perry also had another unapologetic obsession… oranges. When he and the boys would scope out a group of cute girls at the mall and inevitably chicken out, he was always sipping an

Orange Julius. He chugged Sunkist like he was in a state fair contest. Throw in the munchies, and the calories added up to a portly young man who wore his size-too-small, faded Orange Crush t-shirt way more often than any man should ever wear one piece of clothing. There was even a rumor that Perry had once snuck into the girls' soccer practice. Not for what one might rightly expect, but to steal Ziploc bags full of bright, tangy citrus slices.

"Man, I haven't even gotten past the title," Ben said as he and Perry walked leisurely across Marinara's gaming floor. "I mean, *Back* to the Future?"

"I'm telling you, it's coming man. That shit is real," Perry replied, all wide-eyed and stupid.

"Real?" Ben said, raising an eyebrow. "They ran the time machine on beer and bananas. That would make your step-dad a time traveler."

"Oh, okay. Shit on all my dreams," Perry said. "And by the way, Mark's been a great addition to the family."

They passed a group of kids meticulously counting tickets. Perry casually reached into the plastic cup of tokens he was carrying and hurled a handful at the kids' feet. They all immediately dropped to the ground in a frenzy, voices shrieking and arms flailing as they grabbed wildly for those sweet golden coins. "Oh, did you get your shift covered for tomorrow morning?" Perry asked.

Ben took a long second and just looked at Perry, amused at how amused his friend was with his own shenanigans. "No. Couldn't get it covered, but I at least traded so I don't have to open. I'll live."

"Two Advil and a fresh orange. It'll cure everything except for the beer-shits." Perry then lowered his voice, "Do you get beer-shits?"

Ben quickly changed subjects with a burning question of his own. "Hey, did you remind Sarah about tonight?" he asked.

"Yes, she's still coming," Perry said. "Just the fact that she'd show up for this shit-storm tonight should tell you all you need to know."

"I know, I know," Ben replied, although he didn't actually know, know. He'd been head over heels for Sarah since grade school. Ben thought she was the kind of girl that was too good for any guy, except she didn't know it, which of course made her even more perfect. Because of that, Ben never considered himself worthy of her affections, no matter how many signs his friends assured him that she gave. He would never know the answer unless he made a move, and that was tonight, only a decade in the making.

"Ben, you've been waiting years for the right moment. She wants to bone, I know it," Perry said.

Ben winced at the crudeness, but his curiosity was piqued. "Did she say something?" he asked.

"Not answering that," Perry replied as if the question had been asked a hundred times before. He had been around for about as long as Ben had known Sarah and had devoted more than his fair share of life hours indulging Ben in his crush.

Sarah had always loved to swim, so it was no coincidence that Perry and Ben made their way to the community center pool on those hot middle school summer days, even though neither one looked particularly good without a shirt on. Ben would wear his coolest sunglasses and puff his chest out while walking around the pool one too many times. Perry had nothing to lose. He was perfectly content with hotdogs and cannonballs and the occasional dared belly flop from his adoring grade school fans below. Every now and then Ben would recall the smell of chlorine dusted with Doritos, and it would bring him right back to those carefree days.

In high school Sarah became a member of the swim team. Ben wanted to try out, but between his puny shoulders and two left feet he figured it would be a lost cause—that and he couldn't swim for shit. But he would show up to Sarah's meets to support her whenever he could, fully unaware of just how much it meant to her.

As Perry and Ben walked past the ball pit and tube maze, Perry nonchalantly hurled in two handfuls of tokens. Every kid in the vicinity dove in violently, like a pack of starving piranhas who had just found dinner in the rainbow-colored water.

"Look, you two just get really drunk, then…" Perry paused for dramatic effect, then chaotically started thrusting his pelvis back and forth. "It's that easy," he said

"No shit," Ben replied, bending down to pick up an errant token and handing it to a little kid.

"I've heard it's that easy anyway. I've seen a movie where it was that easy," Perry said.

"Good talk," Ben said, patting his friend on the back.

"Agreed. Now we focus on the situation at hand. Let's see it," Perry said, and the two walked to a discreet area.

Ben took the backpack off his shoulder that Keaton had dropped off earlier and set it on a broken Space Invaders arcade. He pulled out the giant bottle of Jack and held it up as if he were one of the prize models on The Price is Right. Perry's eyes were like saucers.

Then Ben got serious for a moment. "I just don't know if he's gonna go for this," he said with worry creeping into his voice.

"He already said he would!" Perry replied. "That'll last him lunch breaks at least a week."

"I'm gonna have to mop up bathroom explosions for a year to pull this off," Ben said.

Perry slapped him on the shoulder. "You already do. Now step up Benji."

Perry pointed to the bottle of Jack. "Just put that in his hand…" He dug into his pocket and pulled out a fresh joint. "And put this in the other. He'll accept. If he's of sound mind he'll accept."

Just then, Perry's eyes and focus drifted off to something wonderful lurking behind Ben. "Wait, wait, this is my guy…"

Ben turned around to see a chubby little kid in matching red sweats dancing to the music from a Mario Bros arcade. Perry wound up like a pitcher and lightly hurled a handful of tokens, hitting the kid in his back mid-boogie. The kid winced and then excitedly dropped to his knees when he saw the bounty at his feet. Ben watched the entire scene unfold. With his hands at his sides, he let out a deep sigh like a parent who was more disappointed than mad. He couldn't help but chuckle though. It was funny as hell.

Ben handed the joint back to Perry. "Keep this. I'm going for it." He zipped the bottle of whiskey in the backpack and began walking towards The Janitor's office.

Perry held up his cup-o-coins and shook it loudly. "C'mon, one more! I saved the best for last!"

"Tell me how it works out," Ben shouted back.

31

Perry tilted his chin up, then strutted over to the women's bathroom. He reached into his chalice one last time, unfurling a smile so sly it would have made The Grinch envious. With his back to the door, he mule-kicked it open and threw a handful of tokens over his shoulder. A horde of stampeding children charged into the restroom as the screams of startled women echoed from inside.

"How excruciating," Perry whispered deviously.

His eyes then caught sight of the stage in the dining pit. "Oh, show's about to start." He plopped the cup of remaining tokens on top of a coin dispenser and turned towards the pit. A new group of naïve, young prospectors immediately surrounded the coin dispenser and jumped hopelessly for the just-out-of-reach cup. Perry's parting gift was his final little victory.

The countdown clock above the stage crept closer to another show. Although Perry came to Marinara for the free games, male bonding and mischief, he always stayed for the band. There was just *something* about them.

CHAPTER FOUR

The dining pit in front of the stage was filled with long, cafeteria-style tables. They were that unmistakable, dull-colored orange that suggested they were purchased from a grade school in the midst of a long overdue renovation. Over-caffeinated children celebrating their Rainbow Brite and Transformers themed birthday parties intermingled and admired one another's cone hats and party favors. For a fleeting moment though, right before the band began its hourly performance, the screaming hoards put down their pizza slices, and a rare hush fell over the room. All eyes were fixated expectantly on the same spot high above the stage.

Hanging there was a digital countdown clock with glowing white numbers. A metal, military-style speaker was crudely rigged to its side. From it boomed the pre-recorded voice of the show announcer who sounded like a cheesy, overly enthusiastic game show host from weekday morning television.

The stage itself was old and rickety. The wooden floorboards were riddled with scuffs from kids who were not supposed to climb onstage but did anyway. Red velvet curtains in need of a good dusting hung heavily from either side, meeting tentatively in the middle as if awaiting that wondrous draw back before each show.

"Five, four, three, two, one…" the speaker voice counted down, joined in unison by a hundred tiny voices. "It's showtime!"

Spotlights began to flicker and dance spontaneously across the red curtains. "And now, Marinara proudly presents: the moguls of mozzarella, the sultans of sauce, the harbingers of heartburn—Meaty and the Toppings!"

Just then, the curtains whipped open and revealed the animatronic band whose reputation always preceded them. The pit was once again completely silent save for an occasional gasp or squeal from an awestruck child. The band stood motionless at first, as if allowing the young audience a chance to marvel at them and soak in their greatness.

Gus Gorgonzola was a stout, white-haired possum who bore more than a passing resemblance to an old country farmer with his big straw hat and a banjo in hand. He had an air of determination about him that was hard to put your finger on, but something in his oddly sadistic expression let you know he meant business.

Alfie Alfredo was a slender, black-haired wolf who donned a black pinstripe suit and played the bass. He exuded ferocity with his gangster-esque attire, sharp fangs and steely glare.

Polly Parmesan was a white-feathered, female duck clad in a preppy, 50's style sweater and poodle skirt. She had a pink satin scarf tied around her neck and layered-on makeup that looked like it was her first attempt. She held a tambourine and wore a slight grin on her face that gave off an air of mischief.

And finally, there was the leader of the pack—Meaty. So iconic a figure he didn't even bother with a last name. He was a massive, black-haired hulk of a gorilla with a golden crown atop his head, confidently cocked to one side as if announcing his preeminence over all others. In any other band the drummer would be behind everyone, but in *this* band, he was front and center.

Meaty sat comfortably behind his drum set while the other bandmates stood for eternity. He was a king atop his throne, akin to the dominant male lion who allows the lesser members of the pride to do the dirty work until he's absolutely needed. But when the king *is* needed, have mercy on any soul in his path. Meaty was the absolute embodiment of raw strength.

As the crowd watched with bated breath, Meaty's head began to slowly and methodically rock back and forth. "Hey kids, ready to have some fun?"

The question was answered with a chorus of delighted cheers and applause. Meaty smashed down his drumsticks with powerful fury, and the band broke into one of its trademark jams. Every child, even a portly teen pothead in the dining pit, went berserk.

While practically everyone else in the building was having fun in the dining pit, Ben was strictly business. He was still psyching himself up outside The Janitor's office when he decided enough was enough. He took a deep breath and knocked on the door.

Ben heard shuffling on the other side and then a click as the door unlocked from the inside. The Janitor cracked open the door just wide enough to peer out, and the proximity of his face to Ben's betrayed any efforts he may have been making to hide the fact that he'd been drinking. The man's breath reeked of whiskey and unbrushed teeth.

"Whaddaya want Ben?" The Janitor barked. Ben winced as the hot, foul air infiltrated his nostrils. He reached into the backpack and pulled out the neck of the giant bottle inside. The Janitor looked down at the whiskey with hungry eyes and then surveyed the room behind Ben. Once he determined there were no onlookers, The Janitor opened the door just wide enough for Ben to enter and locked it behind them.

"Tonight's the big night," Ben said, thinking that was a pretty good opener while cutting straight to the chase. He held out the bottle expecting The Janitor to immediately grab it, but that wasn't the case. The man just looked down at it like he was studying it, then back up at Ben with uneasy eyes. A thousand silent *pleases* ran through Ben's head as he begged the universe to let this work.

After a few more uncomfortable seconds, The Janitor snatched the bottle and set it under his desk.

"You sure are hell-bent on this aren't ya, kid?" The Janitor asked as he threw a greasy rag over the bottle.

"Well, I do have a lot of people counting on me," Ben replied.

"Countin' on you shit," The Janitor said. "I've been thinking, maybe it's not such a good idea to have your little get-together here."

Ben got that familiar pang of fear in his chest that you get right before a test when you forget to study. *Think, Ben, think. Say something to change his mind. Anything.*

"But we had a deal!" was all he could muster, and it came out sounding more whiney than commanding.

"Yeah, a deal," The Janitor replied. "You know, in all the years I've worked here I've never been alone past dark. I get my work done, or I come in early the next morning. You think that's strange?"

Anxious and in no mood for riddles, Ben couldn't hold back his sarcasm. "That you're afraid of the dark?" he scoffed.

The Janitor turned away from Ben and fixed his eyes on a crack in the wall. "I can't explain it. Just a bad feeling," he said. "They're funny, dontcha think? Bad feelings. People skip plane flights every day because of 'em. Mostly they're wrong, sometimes they're right. Guess I never had the guts to find out."

Ben's polite and patient approach gave way to plain old anger as he started to consider the fact that he may actually have to tell his friends the party was off. "Look, I got your shit, and we had a deal. It's not my problem your drunk ass has irrational fears!" he shouted, almost instantly feeling a little bit bad.

The Janitor's mouth curled into a tight-lipped frown, and he gave a long, hard look at the boy. But Ben held his ground, standing tall and tilting his chin up like his father taught him to do. After an agonizing moment of silence, The Janitor finally broke. "You're right. Deals a deal," he said, then hastily turned around. After briefly rummaging through a drawer, he held up an oversized, ornate silver key and slapped it in Ben's hand. Based on its unique appearance, Ben assumed it was probably the same one used on the day of the grand opening.

The Janitor unlocked his office door. "But if anything's broken on, screwed on or shit on—it's on you," he said, punctuating the warning with a pointed finger.

Ben held the key in hand. He should have been exuberant,

but it just didn't feel quite right. He opened the door, then stopped and turned around. "I'm sorry about what I said. I just wanna come through for everyone."

The constant tension painted across The Janitor's face suddenly softened. Ben gave him a light smile and then started through the door.

"Benny, wait," The Janitor called out. "If you feel it tonight, that bad feeling... it's okay to leave."

Ben paused and looked at him. He managed a small nod, then held up the key. "Thanks."

CHAPTER FIVE

A brilliant, cloud-covered moon cast splashes of pale light on the dirt road as Ben's pickup hurtled down it, kicking up enough gravel to leave a dust storm in its wake. The temperature was a rustling breeze away from warm, and the air felt charged with possibility. Watchful eyes of curious coyotes peered out to investigate as they stood partially hidden in the wild brush. The truck's headlights did just enough to light a path but not quite enough to avoid every pothole and dent in the old country road.

In the truck bed, Keaton, Chrissy, Brad and Perry were embracing the thuds and dips like a janky ride at the fall carnival. Uncharacteristically, Ben was driving a little over the speed limit which could be blamed on either the excitement of the night or the fact that Sarah was beside him in the truck— or both. Whatever confidence Ben was lacking in himself certainly wasn't carried over to his ride though. It was about as shiny and clean as he had ever seen it. Brad had earned that ten bucks.

A thin wire ran from the radio and out the back window to a large, square home stereo speaker neatly fastened above the truck bed. Brad had talked Ben into it under the guise that the cool factor would far outweigh its slightly jerry-rigged appearance. Although it pissed off the neighbors, it was great for field parties and nights like this and only took them one sweaty Saturday afternoon to construct. So while it certainly had its merits, Ben was still never entirely thrilled that he'd given in to his friend's peer pressure—until now. And it was perfect. AC/DC's "Highway to Hell" blared to the point of distortion as the wild things in back howled at the moon.

After taking a sip he wasn't thirsty for, Ben blindly reached out until his can of RC Cola connected with a cup holder. As usual he was the designated driver of the group, which he didn't mind, but between the maxed out stereo and obnoxious drunkards, it took everything he had to stay focused on driving. On top of all that, all Ben wanted to do was sneak sideways glances at his lifelong crush who he could hardly believe was actually on her way, *with* him, to the party *he* was throwing.

A shrill clank resonated as Brad dropped an empty beer bottle onto the truck bed. Ben shot a quick glance over his shoulder and cringed as he saw his friend bite the cap off the next bottle and take the inaugural swig.

"All I'm saying is KISS sucks ass," Brad declared. "I'd rather watch Sesame Street in concert than those assholes."

"I've seen Sesame Street Live!" Keaton proudly revealed.

"I'm not much for KISS' music but I do like their makeup," Chrissy added.

"My point exactly," Brad said.

"I'd rather eat a bucket of dicks than sit through a KISS concert!" Perry blurted out. Chrissy gave him a disgusted look which he instantly felt compelled to dispel. "Not really," he said assuredly. But as soon as Chrissy turned away, Perry eyed Keaton and slowly nodded the confirmation—he would indeed rather eat a full bucket of dicks than endure a KISS concert.

Inside the truck cabin Ben's palms were starting to sweat. He took them off the wheel, one at a time, to covertly wipe them on his jeans. Just then the next song started, and Ben couldn't believe his luck. It was like The Outfield wrote "Your Love" just for them, for that exact space in time. Between the gentle glow of the dash in an otherwise dark cabin and that song, Ben could not ask for anything more. The rest was up to him. *Just say something,* his inner voice shouted.

"I'm really glad you could come tonight," he said, trying to sound casual but feeling fairly certain that he didn't.

"Yeah! Me too," Sarah replied. "Remember the last time we were there together?"

"How could I forget?" Ben said. "My first-grade birthday party. Chad Roark peed his pants."

"Yes!" Sarah laughed heartily, her eyes crinkling with joy at the memory, and Ben made a mental note that this was yet another entry on the list of countless things he loved about her.

Another memory, one that Ben would have rather been forgotten, popped into Sarah's head. "And you got stuck in the tube maze! Your mom had to get you down!"

"Noooo," Ben said sarcastically. "That wasn't *me* crying." He figured he might as well own it, because he knew full well there was no bluffing her.

"Oh… Must have been some other kid," Sarah said with a flirtatious smirk.

Ben felt it in his insides… that feeling you get when you're in a moment with someone. That sensation of being in the midst of creating a memory so special you know right then and there it's going to be one you carry with you forever. They held each other's gaze a second too long for just a simple laugh between friends, and Ben was lost in his perfect world—until a drunk moron started whacking the back window.

"The Stones! Turn that shit up!" Brad yelled while pointing up, as if they couldn't hear him. Sarah smiled and turned the volume knob till "Jumpin' Jack Flash" could be heard from the next town over. Ben turned to Brad with an *I'm gonna kill you* look. Either blissfully unaware, or suddenly very aware, Brad lightened the awkwardness. "The Founder! Taking us to the promised land!" he yelled as he obnoxiously slapped the window one last time before turning back to the others.

Ben's friends had been calling him The Founder ever since elementary school when they learned about Ben Franklin and the Founding Fathers. For some ungodly reason Ben's parents thought it was a good idea to make his middle name Franklin, and so Ben's official full name, known to every teacher, classmate and waiting room patient was, embarrassingly, Benjamin Franklin Cooper.

He had learned to live with the first day roll calls and playful ribbing every time some genius pointed it out to him as if it were the first time he'd heard it. His Mom always said that he was named after a man who accomplished great things and that one day, he too would do something great. Sarah was probably the only person he had ever met who had never once teased him or made fun of it. That was on the list too.

In the rearview mirror Ben caught sight of two distinct scenes that made him regret looking up. Perry was making a downright pitiful yet wholehearted attempt at breakdancing while Brad clapped in rhythm and cheered him on. Try as he might, Perry's beefy body parts couldn't quite keep up with the signals his brain was sending. And that wasn't even the dumbest thing going on back there.

Towards the back, Keaton was taking a piss straight up in the air and letting the wind handle the rest. "Rooster tail!" he proclaimed as Chrissy pleaded for him to sit down. An ill-fated crosswind caused a few rogue droplets to smack Keaton in the face. "Son of a bitch," he said as he wiped off his man-wiz.

Brad curiously looked up at the sky. "Y'all feel rain?" he asked. Nobody said a word.

Well there's something you don't see every day, Ben thought.

Brad stood up in the truck bed, wobbling precariously from a combination of uneven road and a level of inebriation that would disable a lesser man. With outstretched arms he let out an adrenaline-charged, primal yell into the fresh night air. He noticed several empty beer bottles rolling around at his feet and wasted no time snatching them up. Brad stood tall like a heroic quarterback in the pocket and motioned forward to an imaginary receiver. "No, go long. We got this," he said.

"You better not," Chrissy warned as she foresaw the event unfolding.

In the truck cabin, Ben and Sarah were calming their nerves into casual conversation. "So how'd you get the key anyway?" Sarah asked.

"It was a little uncomfortable, but all I had to do was—" Ben saw a bottle fly in front of the truck. "Shit!" he exclaimed. Sarah looked at Ben with a half-confused, half-disturbed look, before putting it all together.

Every group had an unofficial dad or mom. Someone who

would keep stupidity within societal norms, which in turn would keep friends from ending up in a hospital or jail. Everyone had comfort in knowing they could get as obliterated as they wanted, and Ben would get them there in one piece. But sometimes dad had to keep the kids in check.

"Brad!" Ben shouted, knowing exactly who the culprit was without even having to look. As he swerved to miss bottles shattering on the hard earth before him, he turned around to see Brad in his natural element.

"Intercepted! That one's gonna hurt in the film room," Brad said.

"Somebody grab him!" Ben yelled.

Brad stumbled over to the back window, "Hey Benny, learn how to drive!"

Finally, Keaton grabbed Brad's shirt and pulled him down. "Sit down man!" he said.

Brad dropped like a sack of potatoes and turned to Keaton, slurring. "Wanna know what I think about KISS and their crazy tongues?"

"What?" an annoyed Keaton asked.

Brad learned across him, and with the top half of his body hanging over the edge, he barfed all down the side of Ben's beloved, fresh-waxed truck.

"Oh my God," Chrissy cried out. "It smells!"

Brad continued to hang upside down, the wind blowing in his face and spattering errant chunks. "I'll clean that," he softly muttered.

Perry looked up from where he was crouched in the far corner of the truck bed smoking a joint. "Are we there yet?"

A few minutes later, and not a moment too soon, Ben took

44

a sharp left and emerged into the parking lot of the promised land. Sarah turned down the music and glanced at the digital clock on the radio which read 9:05 p.m. The night was young.

Ben parked in the last row at the far end of the lot and killed the engine. It was more by habit than by design. He had once gotten door dinged parking close to the building, and once was more than enough. He had learned his lesson in a lot where every car had at least one child carelessly swinging open a door.

Everyone jumped out of the truck carrying something to contribute to the night. Keaton grabbed his backpack that held a small army's worth of liquor. Brad hoisted a giant, silver, double-cassette boom box on his shoulder. The girls teamed up to carry a case of Budweiser which wasn't necessarily the favorite, but it was the cheapest of three choices at the local pit stop. Then there was Perry. They say the best gifts come in small packages, and he had four little rolled presents in his pocket that were gonna last all damn night.

"Why'd you park all the way out here?" Keaton asked.

"I didn't want anyone seeing the truck right in front of the building," Ben said. While that was a partial truth, he just thought he'd leave out the whole door ding phobia thing.

"Good thinking," Keaton said, patting Ben on the back.

A stray but handsome tabby cat slunk around the edge of the parking lot, his green eyes intently watching the group of new people assemble in front of the truck. As everyone else paraded towards the building, Sarah held back. She crouched down and motioned for the little cat to come over, but he stopped just short of the edge, never stepping a paw onto the black asphalt. He began restlessly pacing back and forth across the tall, unkempt grass that lined the property, not once taking his eyes off of her.

45

"I can't come to you. I have to go inside," Sarah said. She waited a few more seconds. "Oh well. You have a nice night okay," she said as she got up to walk towards the building. The handsome stray abruptly stopped pacing and sat. It seemed all he could do was watch.

With a sense of satisfaction he'd never quite felt before, Ben pulled out the coveted silver key and slid it into the front door. It had all been leading to this, and here they were. He looked over his shoulder with a self-assured grin. "Alright, you ready?

Local Arcade-Pizzeria Grand Opening

New restaurant Marinara offers up a carnival-like indoor space where kids can unwind and parents can eat up.

The whispers around town have been building for a little over two decades: What is that grey, square building off Old Mill Road, and will it ever open? Well today we all got our answers in the form of eight, neon red letters.

It was a sublime seventy-five degrees and sunny. A most picturesque day for a grand opening, save for the peculiar group of dark clouds that seemed to hover over the building most of the afternoon.

Owner and founder Silas Skaggs was less exuberant than one might expect on a day like this. He exuded more of a nervous anticipation, which would be more than justified from a man who had poured everything he had into a project spanning roughly a quarter century. Asked about the length of time it took him to open, Skaggs had this to say: "This is a family business. It wasn't put up in a day like some of those other corporate chains. No, this was laid brick by brick. Built by hand right down to that robotic band on stage."

The robotics Mr. Skaggs was referring to are undoubtedly the stars of the show. In a place touting fine Italian fare, video arcades, and an amusement playland, the unique band is what truly sets his restaurant apart. Meaty and the Toppings are technically automatons or animatronics. Basically life-like robots that move and act like flesh and blood creatures. They can talk, sing, and dance, all to the marvel of their young, adoring crowd.

Skaggs views the band as a game-changer, and so does his son who was on hand for the festivities, readily carrying out his father's every instruction. Asked if his son was on the fast-track to management Skaggs said, "He will start as the janitor and work his way up just like everyone else."

The only hiccup on an otherwise perfect day was during the unveiling of the animatronic band. As they powered up for their first performance in front of an audience, all electricity went out in the building. The timing of the outage was impeccable as a news crew was broadcasting live, causing dead air and forcing the station to cut away to another story.

Eventually the band played on. As for the most important guests and potential future customers, the children didn't seem to mind the snafu one bit. And if their enthusiasm is at all telling of the future, Marinara will have a lasting impact for generations to come.

CHAPTER SIX

Ben slowly opened the front door to Marinara, and the group eagerly stepped forward into the darkened lobby. Crossing the threshold, they all immediately felt the teenage rush of being somewhere they knew they shouldn't be.

Just enough soft moonlight eased through the glass door to illuminate their excited faces, but they could see no further. Beyond that was a mysterious gift waiting to be opened. There was nowhere to look other than at one another, and each lock of the eyes ramped up the anticipation even more.

Using the silver key, Ben bolted the door shut. He turned back around and continued to eagerly wait with the others before remembering he was the host. "Oh, hold on one minute," he said, jogging down the hallway and out of sight. He entered a small room with two metal boxes on the wall. Duct tape unevenly labeled each of them, with "power" scrawled on one and "circut breaker" misspelled on the other. As Ben opened the box labeled power, its tight hinges released a harsh metallic screech that assaulted his ears.

Inside was an archaic "knife switch" power lever, similar to something Dr. Frankenstein might have used to activate his great experiment. It took a little muscle to pull down the stubborn copper lever, then a buzz of electricity was heard as Marinara was methodically brought to life. Ben jogged back down the hallway feeling truly satisfied as he saw his friends' expressions.

"Are you serious?" Brad whispered under his breath, his eyes full of wonder as the hum of countless machines whirring to life filled the air with an undercurrent of energy. Everyone at the party had been to Marinara many a time, but something about this time was different. Whether it was the rose-colored glasses of intoxication, the high stakes risk of getting caught or the sheer potential for a night of epic proportions, something intangible made it feel like the first time for all of them—like they were seeing the place through a new pair of eyes.

The group promptly set down their supplies on the first counter they came to. Chrissy hopped up on the ledge, her legs swinging back and forth like a little girl as she popped her Bubble Yum. Keaton unloaded his backpack, taking out six shot glasses and lining them up on the counter. He pulled out a bottle of old faithful and splashed an ounce into each vessel, handing them off one by one as he went. "Ben gets the first toast of the night," Keaton announced.

"Nah, someone else do it," Ben said with an aw-shucks expression.

"No man. First of all, none of this would be happening if it weren't for you. And secondly, I know you hate giving toasts," Keaton ribbed.

"Okay, well…" Ben said as he struggled for words.

"Take your time," Keaton reassured. "You got this."

"Well, even though Brad already puked on my truck and

you my friend practically pissed yourself…" Ben began.

"I did not!" Keaton interjected as the group burst into laughter.

Ben glanced down and let the next words come straight from his heart. "I already know this is gonna be one of the best nights of my life…"

He lifted his head and looked at all the special people surrounding him. "And I hope it's one of yours too."

Keaton proudly raised his glass, and the others followed suit. "To the best night of our lives!" he toasted, and they all tossed back the whiskey with an assortment of grimaces.

Perry turned on the boombox sitting next to them on the counter. He rotated the knob through several stations, but they were filled with static. He reached into his back pocket and pulled out a cassette, overenthusiastically shoving it in his friends' faces with no regard for their personal space. The poor handwriting on the label read: BAD. ASS. SHIT.

Perry slid the tape in and pressed play. The fuzzy, between-song hiss suddenly burst into the hypnotic opening beat of "One Night in Bangkok," the one by Murray Head *not* Robey.

They had booze, they had music and Ben knew the final piece they needed to really get the party started. He headed over to the prize counter and dipped below it for a moment. He popped back up, holding three huge plastic cups overflowing with tokens and clanked them down on the counter. "Oh shit!" Perry said with eyes glazed over.

Brad and Keaton were the first ones over to swoop up the fullest cup and make a beeline to the Pop-A-Shot basketball game. While Keaton's shot still had a certain degree of finesse for a drunkard, he was no match for a moving hoop. In the next lane, Brad was actually *avoiding* his hoop, chunking balls like a caveman at the backboard as hard as he could. He was already embodying what the girls referred to as his "destructo" mode or what the guys referred to as his "son of a bitch" mode. Chrissy sauntered over to cheer them on and slapped Keaton's ass for encouragement. After all, he did look damn good missing shots in that denim jacket.

On the other side of the gaming floor, Sarah and Perry were embroiled in a fierce match of skee-ball. Their competition had amassed a small mountain of tickets between their two alleys, although Sarah's methods of achievement were somewhat questionable. While Perry bowled the brown, wooden balls with perfect form and overzealous focus, Sarah simply tossed each one up to her secret weapon—Ben, who was awkwardly perched atop the lane and dropping in high score after high score. Perry soon became disenchanted, and in a stirring act of sportsmanship, he took his remaining skee-balls and simulated taking a dump on the floor before bidding the lovebirds adieu.

After a while, the group found themselves reconvened at the prize counter. They were all counting and cashing in their tickets, as if abiding by the rules really mattered when they each had unlimited access with the five-finger discount. But there was something to be said for the ritual they had all partaken in since they were kids. The coveted pursuit of those perforated paper rectangles was an ingrained instinct, and they relished it.

The budding couples giggled and flirted while trying on plastic rings, sunglasses and bracelets. The youthful display of teen courtship was juxtaposed with Brad donning an uncomfortably Hitler-esque mustache while pouring a half dozen bags of Pop Rocks into his open mouth. Next to him was Perry, seizing a once-in-a-lifetime opportunity as he shamelessly stuffed his pockets to the brim with Chinese finger traps.

Chrissy had fastened a candy necklace around her neck that Keaton wasted no time stealing a bite of. She grabbed his hand and pulled him along as they headed towards the ball pit and tube maze.

"Look, Runts!" Sarah said as she picked up a box of the hard but not *too hard* fruit flavored candy.

Ben had a special place in his heart for Runts, especially the little banana ones. He and Sarah had Current Events together last year, the only class the two ever had in all of their high school careers, and Ben soaked up every minute. It was his golden hour. Sarah liked the class too but was vocal in her discontent for politics—she just couldn't understand how people weren't able see one another's side.

Current Events was right after lunch, and like clockwork, every single day Sarah would walk in right as the bell rang with a box of Runts. She didn't like the banana ones, so she would sneak them to Ben who loved them. Funny thing though, on the few days a year when Ben would be absent, Sarah would eat the whole box.

While Ben loved Runts because of Sarah, it was a handful of Tootsie Rolls he grabbed before they left the prize counter. The cylinder-shaped chocolate imposters had actually grown on him, mainly because they were one of the only officially sanctioned all-you-can-eat candies at Marinara. Inventory manager Darcy didn't care how many went missing; they were cheap, and kids only used them as filler anyway for their last couple tickets after getting what they really wanted.

Perry had aimlessly wandered over to a Pac-Man table arcade and plopped down on one of the chairs. He started breaking up a nugget of weed on top of the glass, separating it into a line that perfectly matched a path on the screen below. He didn't put in a token but instead chose to watch preview screen after preview screen. Perry experienced the sweaty highs and lows of a high stakes gambler as the little yellow ball with chronic munchies got killed off by ghosts, over and over, without ever randomly reaching hashish highway. After a while, *a long while*, he clinched his fist in silent victory as Pac-Man made his way over to inhale *almost* as much weed as Perry already had.

Ben and Sarah were walking by when Perry motioned for them to come witness greatness at his Pac-Man table. Ben spotted the copious amount of weed and casually veered Sarah in the other direction, instead pointing it out to Brad who gave an affirmative salute and immediately took his marching orders over to the arcade.

****

Keaton and Chrissy were working their way through the seemingly endless tangle of winding, yellow tubes that sat atop the ball pit. The labyrinth was a challenge even for adults as it dwarfed anything found at a golden arches playground or arcade-pizzeria competitor. It was cramped and musky and hot as they crawled through, but that only added to the growing sexual tension between them.

After a couple of wrong turns and a minute of wondering if they'd ever get out, they emerged from the highest of two yellow tubes that opened directly over the pit and took a deep breath of fresh air. They were about to jump when Keaton spotted Brad down below and instinctively threw his arm in front of Chrissy, his eyes wide in horror.

"Brad!" Keaton yelled, his big, inquisitive eyes indicating the asking of a question without words.

After a moment of deciphering his friend's distressed facial expressions, Brad remembered. He shook his head and smiled, giving an all clear thumbs-up. He had not *yet* taken a dump in the ball pit.

Keaton sighed with relief.

"What was that all about?" Chrissy asked.

"You don't wanna know," he replied.

The two counted down in glee— "Three, two, one!" then jumped out of the tube and landed with a splash in the multi-colored ball pit below.

Ben and Sarah had found their way to a Paperboy arcade, and Sarah crossed her arms as she leaned up against it. "Did I tell you I'm the best ever at this game?" she asked, her voice and expression both so full of confidence that Ben found it disarmingly adorable.

"Well, someone should have let this guy know then," he said, pointing to the screen with a raised brow and a rascal's smirk. Every single high score, number one through ten, flashed B-E-N as if broadcasting a warning message to anyone who dare try to challenge the man behind the initials.

"No way!" Sarah said, shoving Ben. "Nerd!"

He shrugged. "I've got a lot of time on my hands."

"Impressive. Sad, but impressive. Guess I'll have to crash the party," she said as she dropped a token into the slot. Ben watched intently as the little pixelated paper boy tossed little pixelated papers at mailboxes, all while dodging rogue lawnmowers, sidewalk breakdancers and runaway tires. After shaking off the rust and some coaching from Ben, Sarah had made it all the way to Thursday. Advancing to Friday, however, was looking futile when Ben noticed Keaton out of the corner of his eye, sitting alone and slumped up against the skee-ball game. Sarah looked up from the screen. "Is he alright?" she asked.

"Yeah," Ben said. "Looks like the deep thoughts part of the night. Mind if I go say hi?"

"Of course," Sarah said, still fully occupied with her game. "Go ahead. I'll be around."

Ben grabbed his beer. "And just in case you haven't done the math, it's gonna take you another hour just to break into the tenth spot."

As Ben walked up, Keaton let out a melancholy "hey" and slapped the floor beside him.

"Where's Chrissy at?" Ben asked, not quite ready to commit to sitting.

"Oh, I told her I just needed a minute," Keaton replied. That was the informal invitation for a talk, and according to friend-code Ben could no longer refuse. He sat down and was immediately passed a bottle of Jack. "You ever think about time?" Keaton asked. "And how you arrive at a place and moment just by random, perfect chance?"

Ben couldn't help but let his mind wander back to Sarah and how tonight was their random, perfect chance. "Yeah, heavy stuff," Ben replied.

Keaton was always the first one out of the group to get philosophical and slow a speeding night down. But it was cool. The drinking and debauchery were where the memories were made. But this was where the bonds were forged.

"Quite a night so far," Keaton said. "You did good Benny. The Founder delivered."

Ben raised the bottle in silent appreciation and took a short swig. It didn't happen often, but it always felt good to get a genuine compliment from a friend. Nothing was said for a while after that. Their eyes both drifted into the distance, lost in thought and comfortable in their quiet camaraderie.

The two had been friends for as long as Ben could remember. They met on their second-grade field trip to the zoo and became instant buddies when they both got thrown in detention for flinging bananas from their sack lunches into the monkey cage. Both still had the matching plastic monkey molds they'd made that day on the Mold-A-Rama machine as a stinky, tar-smelling memento.

They maybe weren't best friends but they were good friends, and that friendship had stood the test of time. As they grew up, Keaton got popular with the girls, which in turn meant he got popular with everyone, and they started to run in different circles and sit at different lunch tables. But through it all, they remained pals. Keaton always invited Ben to the cool kids' parties, which Ben usually declined but always appreciated.

Keaton never changed, just the circumstances around him did, and as long as he treated Ben the same it would always be good. Besides, it certainly had its benefits. Having an insider to introduce you to the cheerleaders and captains of the football team was never a bad thing. Ben even became unlikely friends with a certain rambunctious quarterback and gum chewing blonde because of Keaton's introductions. So while everyone in the group hailed from different social circles and perspectives of the high school experience, they all had one thing in common. They were wise enough to realize that, at the end of the day, labels were just that—bullshit.

"So, what's up with Sarah?" Keaton asked, snapping Ben out of his reverie.

"It's actually going pretty good," Ben said. As the words came out, they were as much news to him as they were to Keaton. He had been so caught up in the night that he hadn't yet had a chance to self-analyze and overthink every detail.

Wow. It actually is *going pretty* good, Ben thought. His next realization was that he wasn't talking things up, and it might be time to pinch himself to make sure it was all real.

Keaton raised one of his perfectly shaped eyebrows. "Now you know I love you, so I can say this, but facing adversity's never been your strong suit."

"Won't argue with that," Ben admitted.

"Tonight can be that first step to you reaching deep down inside and finally saying... fuck it, what do I got to lose?" Keaton said.

"Is that the liquor talking?" Ben quipped.

"You know I'm a sentimental drinker," Keaton replied, a slight slur creeping into his words. He motioned his head towards Sarah who was now over by the prize counter trying to work a plastic wind-up 'radio.'

"There she is right now, trying to work a toy radio," Keaton said, and they both laughed. "But seriously, no regrets tonight brother." Ben nodded and Keaton gently shook the bottle in front of him. "Liquid courage."

Ben took one last swig. "Good talk," he said, pushing himself up.

"Always. Now go get your girl," Keaton said, slapping Ben on the ass as he walked away. "The stars are aligned!"

Once Ben was gone Keaton completely zoned out on a random spot on the wall. As he stared ahead in a vapid stupor, his body gradually started leaning to one side until he slumped down to the floor, the bottle of Jack tipping over along with him.

At first he couldn't tell if he was imagining things when he heard the strange noise, but after making a determined effort to concentrate, Keaton realized he was indeed hearing it. "Do you guys hear that?" he whispered with his head against the ground. But nobody was around to listen. The noise was unusual, something he had never heard before. It wasn't continuous as there was more of a rhythmic flow to it, like ocean waves rolling onto shore. But unlike the comforting sounds of nature which had their place in this world, this had an underlying negativity to it.

Keaton's expression went from confused intrigue to unease, and a sudden feeling of cold anxiety coursed through his veins, counteracting the warm buzz of the alcohol. He closed his eyes tightly and pressed his ear against the floor as he strained to hear it again, but there was nothing, just a slow heartbeat. So he told himself it was just his intoxicated psyche playing tricks. By the time the noise happened again, almost so faint one couldn't hear it, Keaton was snoring.

CHAPTER SEVEN

The rotating bucket seat ride was not a fan favorite of anyone over the age of three, but tonight Perry was the hard exception to the rule. While everyone else was having an absolute blast, Perry was just plain blasted. He had somehow stuffed his XL man-body into the kiddie bucket seat and was stressing the limits of the motor as he circled slowly no more than five feet off the ground. Sporting a tiny pair of children's sunglasses and a joint that clung to his bottom lip, Perry sat motionless, his mind skipping in a field of tranquil indifference.

While Keaton and Perry had both succumbed to the influence of their poisons and almost mellowed to a halt, Brad was still raging like a caged beast. After channeling Bruce Lee and repeatedly knocking the complete shit out of a children's test-your-might punching bag, Brad moved on to greener pastures. He had been obliterating the poor little plastic creatures on a homemade Whack-A-Mole game for a good while, but one seemed to keep evading him. As the little brown varmint taunted his manhood, Brad considered walking away, when a way better idea struck him. He delicately set the attached rubber mallet down, not once taking his eyes off his cunning adversary. Like a savant counting cards, Brad's eyes darted around the table as he studied the routine of the particularly googly-eyed mole. Then he grabbed a bottle of Jack and shattered it all over the little dude.

Back at the skee-ball lanes, Keaton had almost been down for the count—that is, until Chrissy roused him with a few select whispered words. They were now at the air hockey table, nearing the end of an epic blowout where the digital scoreboard read 6–0. Keaton looked up, lamenting the last fifteen minutes of his life. *The things I do for a decent hook up*, he thought.

He held his sombrero-shaped plastic paddle in place, unmoving, as Chrissy aimlessly smacked the puck willy-nilly all over the table. Keaton went to his Zen place as the puck made contact everywhere and anywhere but the actual goal—until he couldn't hold back any longer. With one effortless swipe, he smacked the puck swiftly into the opposing goal. 7–0. Game over.

"For real?" Chrissy said.

"I swear, I'm not even trying," Keaton replied.

"Okay fine. One more game?" Chrissy asked.

Keaton tried not to let his expression betray his sincerest attempt to hide the fact that he was in actual hell. Just then, he noticed Ben crossing the game floor beside Sarah who was carefully fastening a plastic, pink watch around her wrist, and he seized his chance at salvation. "Hey!" he called out. "You two versus me and Gretzky."

Sarah looked up from her newly acquired accessory. "Sounds fun," she said.

"Alright!" Keaton said, more relieved than excited. "Losing team has to chug a beer."

Ben hesitated, but Sarah turned to him. "Oh come on. We can take 'em!" she said, and Ben caved, as he now knew he always would whenever Sarah looked at him with that hopeful glimmer in her eye.

"Okay," Ben said, and they took their places at one end of the table. "I've got five minutes to wipe the floor with this guy."

"You're a funny guy Benny," Keaton said, doing his best attempt at a bad Arnold impression. "I like you. That's why I'm going to kill you last." Ever the showman, Keaton placed the puck on the table, teasing telegraphed strikes as the air lightly hovered it in place. Ben rolled his eyes but couldn't hide his amused grin, because he knew that's what friends did—they screwed with each other.

Keaton drew back and mercilessly whacked the puck with all the testosterone-fueled fury he'd been waiting to unleash since his last game with Chrissy. The puck shot down the table in a blur and clunked into the goal before Ben or Sarah could even manage a swipe at it. "Get ready to guzzle kids, it's gonna be a long night!" Keaton said. Ben and Sarah stood in silence, trying to figure out what the hell happened as the puck popped out the bottom of their side. "Why the long faces guys? There are no losers in drinking games!" Keaton exclaimed.

"Be nice Keaton," Chrissy said. "No more slap shots."

"Fair enough," Keaton said, having the satisfaction of knowing full well after that first goal that he could beat them two-on-one if he wanted.

"Hey, where are the guys at?" Ben asked, suddenly noticing Brad and Perry had been absent from the festivities for some time.

"I've been wondering the same thing," Keaton said.

Perry hadn't moved a muscle and was still rotating around in the bucket seat, seemingly frozen in his welcomed incoherent state. The only difference was that Brad was now there, standing a few feet away and silently observing his spaced-out friend. As Perry's seat circled around, Brad strategically held out his index finger and waited. Perry didn't even flinch as Brad's burly finger squished into his face, but he did crack an ever so slight smile as the bucket seat continued its rotation. "You got fingered," Brad deadpanned, then quickly buried his nose in his forearm with a grimace. "Oh my God! What's wrong with your *ass*?" he said as he bent over, dry heaving.

Back at the air hockey table the score was 3–3, and Keaton and Chrissy had possession of the puck. "I'm getting tired of this," Chrissy said, giving Keaton a pout that had no doubt worked for her many times in the past.

"Okay, okay, how about next shot wins?" Keaton announced, taking full advantage of the fact that it was his turn to shoot.

"That's fine with me," Sarah said. "I feel like it's only a matter of time before I walk away from this with a fractured finger the way you boys play."

Brad, having made a full recovery from the killer ass-gas, stumbled over to the table, carrying the giant handle of Jack they'd bribed The Janitor with. "Who's winning?" he asked.

Ben did a double take as he looked up. "Damn it Brad! Is that The Janitor's?"

Brad jerked the bottle close to his chest. "This one tastes better!"

"Where did you get it?" Ben asked.

"I found it left out with a bunch of rags in the dining pit," Brad said, pointing to the tables down below.

"He must've left in a hurry," Ben said.

"I think the old dude was just washin' and sloshin' at the same time!" Brad said.

"Holy shit. I am not pitching in for another one of those," Keaton said.

In an act of drunken defiance, Brad tilted his head back and raised the bottle to his lips, but Ben swooped in just in time and grabbed it away, splashing whiskey all over Brad's shirt. Defeated yet unfazed, Brad gave a gentlemen's nod to his friends, then wandered off like a lumbering oaf to find another libation.

"There's not much gone. Maybe we can fill it up, and he won't know the difference," Sarah said.

"Later," Keaton replied as he got back into battle position at the table. "Let's finish the game."

Ben set the giant bottle of whiskey on top of a nearby arcade. "You might as well grab a couple beers while you're over there and save yourself the time," Keaton said.

Ben walked confidently back to his side of the table. "Bring it."

"You ready?" Keaton asked. "Here it comes!"

He zigzagged the puck down the table, but it was no match for Sarah's laser focus—she wanted it bad. She intercepted the incoming puck and sent it flying straight through the goal. "Yes!" she yelled as she jumped into Ben's arms.

Sarah turned to Keaton and Chrissy. "You guys don't have to chug the beer if you don't want to."

"Oh yes they do," Ben said.

"Thank you, *Sarah*, but rules are rules," Keaton said.

Chrissy and Keaton each grabbed a beer and started the long, hard chug. Keaton, of course, finished first then polished off the rest of Chrissy's after she threw in the towel. He put the two empty cans on the table and, for *mostly* dramatic effect, slumped down to the ground.

"Let's get out of here," Ben whispered to Sarah, who nodded in agreement. "Guys, we're gonna catch up with you in a bit," he announced.

"Okay," Chrissy replied. Only Keaton's hand was visible, still grasping the top of the table. It gave a thumbs-up.

Ben led Sarah to the far side of the gaming floor where a photo booth stood, discreetly tucked away in a corner next to a couple of perpetually out-of-order arcades. "I was thinking a victory picture," Ben said.

"I didn't know they had one of these!" Sarah exclaimed. Ben held back the thin curtain and invited her inside.

"It's kind of a tight squeeze," Ben said as he stepped in.

"We'll manage," Sarah replied.

Ben took his cue to slip one arm around her shoulder as he sat down beside her. Her body felt warm and soft up against his, and he realized this was the closest physically he'd ever been to her. *Keep your cool.*

He gently grazed his head against hers and took a breath of her for the first time. The blend of light perfume on her skin and hair put his senses into a tailspin. *Hold it together.*

His stomach started to get that churning, fluttery feeling, and he wondered if she felt the same thing too.

"Ready?" Ben said as he dropped a token into the slot. "It's gonna flash four straight times."

64

"Okay. Wait! Funny or serious?" Sarah asked.

"Uhh… first two stupid, last two normal," Ben quickly replied. The flashes were abrupt and bright, barely giving them time to adjust poses between captures. Just before the fourth and final photo snapped, Ben and Sarah caught each other's eyes. They held an electric gaze which left an imprint on their souls that would far outlast what the camera had captured on film.

"It takes a minute to come out," Ben said.

"No hurry," Sarah replied, laying her head on his shoulder and closing her eyes.

Her small hand reached blindly for his and found it easily, their fingers interlacing as both of them, in unison, gave the other a gentle squeeze. *Just please… please… be mine forever.*

"What are you thinking?" Sarah quietly asked. Ben saw his perfect moment manifest right there in front him. In some ways it felt like it was all a dream, too perfect to be real, but in other ways it felt like the truest, most predestined moment of his entire life. All he knew for sure was that he wanted it more than anything ever. There was no more wondering, no more doubt and no more insecurity. As nervous as he was, he knew the question *and* the answer, and it was finally time.

"That maybe you should be my girlfriend?" Ben answered. Sarah's relaxed eyes snapped open, and a huge smile spread like warm sunshine across her face.

"I'm thinking yes," she said without hesitation.

"So it's official," Ben said as he leaned back and put his arms behind his head. Sarah blushed at his boyish charm and laid her head against his chest. Unknowing of the other, they both closed their eyes and took it all in, intertwined in perfect happiness.

There was only one thing left to do, and it was unbelievably even more exciting and nerve-racking than what had just transpired over the last couple minutes. "You Might Think" by The Cars started serenading them from the boom box somewhere in the building, and Ben put an endgame to his delaying the inevitable. *This is it. I have to do it before the song is over. Make a move Ben.*

His self-motivational session was interrupted as Sarah looked up at him longingly. "Ben, you were right," she said.

"About what?"

"This is the best night of my life."

The feeling was better than he could have ever imagined. All of a sudden his nerves were gone. The song was almost over. Ben could hear her soft, airy gasp of breath as he leaned in close for the kiss, and in that instant, the world, the universe and Heaven above stopped as their lips touched for the first time.

A bell announced the photos were ready and they got out to eagerly inspect their performances. Sarah took the four-print strip from the metal receptacle it had fallen into.

"Oh my God, look at that face!" she said, pointing to the very first frame and bursting into laughter.

"What?" Ben said. "That's my smiling one!"

"Which one's your favorite?" Sarah asked.

Ben pointed to the last photo, the one that so perfectly captured them gazing at one another. "I'd have to go with this one," he said.

"Mine too," she said. "I don't have any pockets. Would you mind holding onto them?"

"Sure," Ben replied, sliding them into his back pocket and

taking her hand. He could hear the rest of the gang hootin' and hollerin' not too far away. "Let's go somewhere a little more private. I know a spot under the stage where no one will find us."

"Lead the way boyfriend," Sarah said.

CHAPTER EIGHT

Chrissy had managed to rescue Keaton from the brink of oblivion for the second time that night and was now forcing him to do her bidding on the claw machine. A coveted ALF doll was wedged between a Smurf and a Care Bear, and Keaton was on a mission. The metal claw dropped and lightly wrapped itself around ALF's bulbous snout, then rose back up empty handed. "Oh, so close!" Chrissy said.

Keaton looked down into his token cup. "Only three left," he warned as he picked one out and dropped it into the slot. Another swing and a miss went by. "I don't think it's gonna happen tonight sweetie," he said. "Daddy's had a little too much to drink."

"Come on Keaton. I really want an ALF," she pleaded.

"I'm about to ALF all over your shoes if I don't get something to eat," he replied. Chrissy looked down like a scolded puppy, and Keaton gave in. "Okay, I'll try a couple more times. But if I get you a prize, I think I should get something in return," he said.

Chrissy leaned in slightly. "And just what did you have in mind?"

"How about a kiss?" he said. "Size, length and placement completely up to you."

"Fair trade," she replied.

"Lucky for you I've never won anything on this stupid game in my whole life," Keaton said.

Chrissy dropped a handful of tokens into Keaton's cup. "Well, lucky for you, there are a lot of chances."

****

Sarah was still holding tight to Ben's hand when they reached the short set of steps leading up to the wooden platform Meaty and the Toppings called home. "Where are we going?" Sarah asked.

"Hold on. Almost there," Ben replied, as they walked up the steps and onto the darkened stage. He lifted the heavy, red velvet curtains, and a light cloud of dust filled the air. They both coughed lightly as they crawled underneath, and the comforting background noise of laughter and music slowly disappeared into absolute silence.

Sarah looked up in the darkness, and a sudden silhouette caught her off guard. As her eyes adjusted, the shadowy, faceless figure began to emerge. It was the pinstripes on the trousers that first came into focus. As she stood up, Sarah realized it was Alfie who had been glaring down at her the whole time.

She was shocked at how realistic he looked up close. "They say the creator used as many real animal parts as possible," Ben said. The black coarse hair and sharp, perfectly opaque fangs looked so convincing that it was easy to believe they were once parts of a flesh and blood living beast.

"Creepy," Sarah whispered, taking it all in. She then looked around and realized she was talking to herself.

"Over here," Ben said. Sarah walked behind the band to the middle of the stage where he was knelt down searching for something.

Ben ran his hand across the old floorboards until he connected with a small, drilled hole that he put his finger through. As he tugged on it, Sarah asked, "What is that?"

"It's a trap door. I heard back in the day before the stage speaker was installed that a live host would come up and introduce the show," he explained. "Not sure whatever happened to him." He also wasn't sure why the door was so abnormally large for such a small stage.

The rickety flap finally gave way and Ben propped it open, exposing a secret, hidden chamber below. "Why are we going down there?" Sarah whispered, a hint of concern creeping into her voice.

"Trust me, I do it all the time," Ben whispered back. "And why are we whispering?"

Sarah shrugged with a laugh and followed Ben as he started down the steps that led to the underbelly of the stage. As dark as the stage was, the underneath was pitch black. Ben flipped a switch, and the room illuminated with an amber glow. Sarah immediately let out a scream and jumped backwards as she found herself inches away from a mutilated Meaty head.

Ben couldn't help but laugh at Sarah's reaction. "I'm sorry. I didn't know it was that close," he said.

"What the hell?" she snapped, playfully pushing him but visibly shaken.

After settling down, curiosity eventually won over and Sarah walked up to the atrocity. The decaying head was sawed off crudely at the neck and impaled haphazardly on a metal pole. The remaining patches of black gorilla hair couldn't keep hidden the dull metal skeleton underneath, and the floor below it was covered with the bristly strands that had fallen out over time. It was missing an eye, and the other was stuck wide open and hanging down as if someone had quit in the middle of prying it loose. The teeth were perfect and complete, but the lips had rotted off, leaving a permanently crazed smile on the creature.

"So this is where they store all the old models and broken parts," Ben said, gesturing his arm widely as if to introduce her to his secret kingdom. The room was cluttered, stale and musty. It was no different from an old basement, but the things *inside* it were very different. Severed limbs of long-retired animatronics were piled high on shelves along with heaps of unusual electrical parts. Old arcades, some in need of repair, some just hollow shells, lined the walls wherever there was any free space remaining.

In a strange display, a few more detached appendages were nailed to the wall, more reminiscent of a hunter's lodge than a family arcade. The most disturbing aspect of the room though was the roughly half dozen impaled versions of The Toppings, purposely placed about as if on display in some macabre museum.

"Pretty cool, huh?" Ben asked.

Sarah was something other than impressed. "Yeah… Why are there so many of them?"

71

"Not sure. There's a show every hour on the hour, seven days a week though. Things wear out I guess."

"Hmm," she said, wandering around and inspecting the oddities of the room.

"I hide in here sometimes," Ben said, pulling on a tarp that was covering something big and bulky on the floor. A giant bean bag was revealed which he promptly jumped backwards into. "I'll take naps, sneak food. Beats cleaning toilets."

He reached out his hand and pulled Sarah down to cozy up next to him. With a single shared look they made a silent agreement to skip the small talk and get straight to the good stuff.

As they were making out, the loud sound of wood slamming into wood startled them out of their moment. Sarah shot straight up, her eyes wide with distress. "It was just the door," Ben reassured her, but she was not comforted.

"Can we go?" Sarah asked, looking nervously around the room.

"Well sure, but—"

"Shh, do you hear that?" she said.

They both slowly tilted their heads up and listened carefully. The faint twang of a slow, bluegrass tune drifted softly down from the stage above. "Is that a banjo?" Sarah asked hesitantly. As she finished her sentence, the music stopped.

"It's just the guys messing around," Ben said, trying his best to convince them both. He looked up and shouted, "Guys! Cut it out!"

Sarah abruptly stuck her hand out to silence Ben. "No," she whispered. "Look up."

The wood beams in a small area of the ceiling slightly bowed and made an awful creak as dust gently floated down. Shortly after, about three feet away from where it had first appeared, dust fell again. It happened one more time then stopped. There was so much dust suspended in the room that it looked like apocalyptic fallout. The sequence definitely fit a familiar pattern, but there was a problem—there had been no sound of footsteps entering the stage. Perhaps even more unsettling, there had been no sound of any leaving it either. "Could the guys do that?" Sarah asked.

"I'm about to find out," Ben said as he stomped up the stairs. He burst through the trap door and climbed out onto the stage. His eyes darted quickly back and forth, assessing every shape and shadow in the darkness, but there was no one to be seen. Ben hastily pulled back the stage curtains, fully expecting one or more of the guys to be standing there belly laughing, but there was no one there. "Very funny guys," he yelled out over the dining pit. "You got us!"

Sarah came up beside him and put a hand on his arm. She looked back at the band members standing ominously in the dark.

The prank had gone too far Ben thought, but he wasn't going to let it ruin the night. "I'll bash heads later," he said. "You hungry?"

Sarah looked at him, trying to mask her nerves. She mustered a small smile. "Yeah," she replied.

"Then let's go," Ben said.

While attempting to keep their cool, they both walked with unmistakable haste down the stairs and far away from the stage.

CHAPTER NINE

While other areas of Marinara may have been showing their age, its industrial kitchen was oddly pristine. All the surfaces and appliances were stainless steel, and a huge countertop island dominated the center of the room. Ben and Sarah walked up to the kitchen's large flapping door and peeked through the rectangular plastic window to spy on whoever was inside. They snickered when what they saw lived up to expectations. Over his t-shirt, Perry was wearing a white chef's coat with the ridiculous, matching tall hat. He was hovering inches over an uncooked pizza and inspecting it with a striking combination of smug approval and intense scrutiny.

Sarah and Ben burst through the door. "Perry!" Sarah exclaimed, like someone tipsy at a party who hadn't seen their friend in over thirty minutes.

"I'm surprised. I would've guessed you raided the kitchen hours ago," Ben said. "By the way, was that you on stage—"

"Shh. My masterpiece is almost complete," Perry said in a hushed museum-voice as beads of sweat slowly trickled down his brow. It was a beautiful piece of pie-art, most closely resembling a meat lovers with scarcely a veggie in sight. He reached for a generous pinch of a dried green herb sitting in a dish and sprinkled it painstakingly over every slice.

"I have a bad feeling that's not basil," Ben said.

Perry gestured to the pizza with a flourish of his wrist. "Weed Supreme will be ready shortly," he announced with the same pride and sense of accomplishment Michelangelo or Monet had no doubt felt ages ago.

All Ben and Sarah could do was politely nod their heads. They all three looked around in awkward silence until Sarah found an escape route.

"This is pretty big," she said, taking in the room in all its shiny, spotless grandeur. "I've never been in a restaurant kitchen before." She walked over to the fridge and opened the door. "So what're we eating?"

"Let's see what we got," Ben said as he snuck up from behind and rested his chin on her shoulder. They looked over the neatly organized shelves, taking their time to assess the many options. Ben pulled out a huge, two-foot tall vat of marinara sauce and lugged it over to the stove.

"That's a lot of sauce," Sarah said.

Ben strained to speak as he set it down. "They make it in bulk."

With Weed Supreme complete, Perry was ready for his next culinary feat. He was hunched over the fryer jiggling knobs when he turned to Ben. "Hey, do you know how to turn this thing on?" he asked.

"I've never used it before. Why?" Ben replied.

"Found some wangs in the freezer," Perry said, holding up a plastic bag of Marinara's finest hors d'oeuvres.

"I don't wanna mess with it," Ben said. "Just use a pan."

75

Perry's nose curled up in disappointment, and he plodded off to find one.

Sarah was over at the counter eyeing a mound of unused pizza dough. "I've always wanted to spin one of these in the air, but I know in my heart it's gonna end up on the floor," she said.

"Then we'll just add a Dirt Deluxe to tonight's menu," Ben quipped. They took turns clumsily throwing the pizza dough in the air and laughing harder than they had all night. After hitting the overhead light, they decided to stop while they were ahead and roll it out. There was enough for two pizzas. "Okay, one for us and one for Keaton and Chrissy," Ben said.

"What about Brad?" Sarah asked.

"He's so drunk I'll tell him Weed Supreme was his idea," Ben said. Sarah's laughter was cut off by the last word anybody wanted to hear in a kitchen.

"Fire," Perry calmly announced, way too nonchalant for the raging inferno that had risen out of the pan in front of him.

Ben looked up. "What the shit Perry! For real?!" He ran to the sink and filled a cup with water. Just as he was about to pour it over the pan, Sarah swiftly interjected.

"Ben!" she yelled, stopping him just in time. She threw a towel over the blazing pan, and the flames quickly died out. "Water on a grease fire, huh? And I ask *you* for help in chemistry?"

Before Ben had time to come up with an excuse, Perry came to the rescue with the most perfectly timed, dumb-ass question. "Can I make some more?"

"No!" Ben and Sarah both yelled in perfect unison.

"He is not allowed around that stove again tonight," Sarah quietly said to Ben.

"Agreed," he replied.

"Hey Perry," Sarah said sweetly, as if she were talking to a young child. "Would you mind finding Brad and setting the table?"

Perry bowed down with his hands clasped in prayer, then headed towards the kitchen door.

****

An eight-foot tall, yellow outline of a square was the entryway to a slide that connected the game floor to the dining pit below. Everyone called it the square slide, and it served as a fun way for kids to get down to the pit in lieu of taking the stairs located right next to it.

Perry had successfully recruited Brad to help him set the table, and they agreed it was a no brainer to take the slide instead of the stairs, even though their arms were piled high with dishes, glasses and cutlery.

"So I'm just about to do it when I see Keaton and Chrissy at the top..." Brad said.

"Taking a dump in a ball pit? That's low-class, even for you," Perry said, and the two slid down without breaking a single dish.

When Perry stood up at the bottom of the slide, he noticed the stage curtains were wide open. The band members were frozen in motion, each one in a different pose but all facing straight forward. "Were those open before?" he asked.

"Ben probably opened them for the show," Brad replied.

They started setting plates and silverware on one of the long cafeteria tables that sat directly in front of the stage.

"Man, it looks like they're watching us. Here, look," Perry said, motioning for Brad to follow him.

The two walked parallel to the stage between the rows of tables. "Creepy. It's like their eyes follow you wherever you go," Brad said.

"This is ridiculous," Perry said nervously, a cold chill seeping its way into his bones.

"Dude, we just learned this in art class. It's an optical illusion, like the paintings at the museum," Brad said.

"Yeah, that's right," Perry said, nodding with relief.

"Let's go get the rest of the stuff," Brad said as he walked towards the stairs. Perry hurried to catch up to his friend, feeling a little foolish but still not wanting to be left alone in the pit.

As the boys made their way up the steps, four sets of eyes followed them with fixated stares until they were out of sight.

After gathering the last of the supplies from the kitchen, Brad and Perry headed back to the pit with napkins, serving utensils and shakers filled with parmesan cheese and pepper flakes. They both stopped dead in their tracks when they reached the top of the stairs. The stage curtains were now closed.

"Those were definitely open," Perry said.

"They've gotta be automatic or something," Brad replied. "We're not that blasted, right?"

"I know I am," Perry said, and they both laughed way longer than if they'd been sober. They put the finishing touches on the table and went back to join the others.

****

The whole group was seated around the cafeteria table with a drunkard's dream smorgasbord lain out in front of them.

Three large pizzas, spaghetti, mozzarella sticks and partially burnt chicken wings made up the menu for the night. It came as no surprise that Ben and Sarah were sitting next to each other, and across from them were Keaton and Chrissy. Brad and Perry each sat next to a couple, more than content to be the third and fourth wheel.

Chrissy decided to start feeding Keaton, and the excessive PDA was eliciting internal eye roles from everyone at the table, especially Keaton. Perry was sporting an official Marinara plastic bib around his neck while peeling the cheese off the slices on his plate and forming a small pile. Brad eagerly reached over for his first slice of pizza and took a big bite.

"How is it Brad?" Sarah asked.

"Tastes like shit," Brad replied through a mouthful of Weed Supreme. "Something's wrong with it."

Perry turned to Brad with his hands clasped in prayer and bowed.

After a few more bites, Brad held out the slice with a scrunched-up nose. "Man, does this smell funny?" he asked, and Ben and Sarah did everything they could to contain themselves, despite being red-faced and nearly bursting at the seams.

Sitting on the outside of an inside joke, Chrissy turned her interest to something under the table. She reached below and pulled out a stuffed doll. "Look what Keaton won me!" she proudly announced.

Perry gleefully uttered a single, semi-audible word through his mouthful of spaghetti, "ALF!"

"You won that from the claw?" Ben asked in partial disbelief. "That greedy box of shit has only let one prize go since I started here. You've given the kids hope again!"

"And it only *didn't* cost me thirty-six dollars' worth of tokens," Keaton said. Chrissy lowered the doll as her focus was diverted to Perry who looked as if he was gnawing on an entire pack of bubble gum, only it wasn't pink.

"I just invented a real-life Everlasting Gobstopper," Perry gloated. He took a greasy wad of cheese out of his mouth to show it off to anyone who would look. "Pizza gum!"

He wrapped it in a white napkin for later use, but almost immediately the cheese grease seeped through, fusing with the napkin and creating what looked like a translucent Chinese dumpling.

Chrissy watched as Brad snatched the chewy gob and stuck it in his own mouth, napkin and all. Her expression became an emotional rollercoaster that took her from complete disbelief to unbridled disgust.

Brad was laughing his ass off at his thievery until the laughing turned into choking. He violently coughed a few times, then regurgitated a wet wad of communal cheese onto the table.

"And he's alright!" Keaton bellowed, handing Brad a glass of water. "Now that's dinner and a show."

"Oh, I almost forgot," Ben said as he stood up and walked away from the table.

"What?" Keaton asked.

"The show!" Ben yelled back.

Brad was now fully recovered from his near brush with death and totally stoked. "Yes!" he said. "Bring those creepy bastards on!"

Keaton turned to Chrissy. "Have you ever seen the show before?" he asked.

"No, never," she replied.

"Oh, you're in for a treat," Keaton said. "Think Showbiz, only shittier."

****

Ben walked to the side of the stage. He sifted through his keychain until he came to a duplicate of a duplicate of a key marked "Do Not Copy." He unlocked a small control panel and flipped the few switches necessary to bring the show to life, just as he'd done a hundred times before. Ben paused for a brief moment, alone for the first time since they'd arrived. He took a deep breath and smiled, then headed back to meet his friends.

****

Ben arrived in the dining pit just in time to hear the voice from the stage speaker make the opening announcement. "Gather 'round boys and girls! The show's about to begin!"

The white digital numbers on the countdown clock were ticking down, and the stage lights began to flicker. "Five, four, three, two, one… It's showtime!" the voice proclaimed, and on cue the red curtains blasted open.

Perry leaned over to Chrissy. "This is gonna change your life."

Meaty, front and center, commanded attention first. His massive head rocked back and forth as his jaw slowly opened for him to speak. "Hey kids. Ready to have some fun?" he said. The six raucous kids with front row seats answered with a loud mix of cheers, boos and a few disgraceful obscenities.

The band broke out into a classic rock song that everyone had heard of but never wanted to hear played that way again. Aside from sounding like it was a cover by the local puppeteering troupe, the unneeded infusion of corny adlibs made it unlistenable to anyone sober over the age of ten, which luckily tonight wasn't a problem.

Slightly under the music, the sound of grinding motors and hydraulics could be heard as the animatronics performed their choppy, mechanical dance moves. Their mouths opened and closed unnaturally, the imitation of speech out of sync just enough from the words on the soundtrack to evoke an unsettling feeling.

"Oh my God. Those are terrifying," Chrissy said.

"They do kinda suck," Perry agreed.

"Come on!" Brad said, clearly very enthused with the performance. "This is the main attraction. They're the elephants of the circus!" He jumped out of his seat and hoisted himself onto the stage.

"Brad, what are you doing?" Chrissy asked.

"Something every red-blooded American boy has always wanted to do," Brad replied as he looked under the skirt of Polly Parmesan. "Disappointing," he said, shaking his head.

Brad headed over to Gus who was moving in place and picking his banjo. He leaned in close, examining the possum's facial features. "You guys should come up here and see these things up close. They look like shit!"

"I don't think so," Sarah said. "Been there, done that."

Brad slapped down on Gus's snout and the impact interrupted its movement ever so slightly. "I could make one of these out of a fur coat and some broomsticks!" he yelled out.

"Just don't break anything," Ben shouted. "They'll take it out of my paycheck."

"You get paid?!" Brad yelled back, wincing as he sniffed under Gus's armpit.

After polishing off his last slice of pizza, Keaton turned from the train wreck on stage to Chrissy. "I'm still waiting on that kiss," he said.

"Don't worry. I plan on paying up," she said, lightly placing a hand on his knee.

Keaton cleared his throat and pushed back from the table. "I can't even look at food anymore," he announced. "I think we're gonna go play some games."

As the two walked away, Perry called out, "Go introduce her to Lyndon Johnson!" then laughed at his own joke.

Sarah turned to Ben, trying to come across like she was making an observation rather than a complaint. "It's really loud," she said.

"Yeah. You guys about done with the band?" he asked.

Perry gave a thumbs-down while making a fart noise, which Ben took as a yes.

"Yeah, turn it off," Sarah said. Ben stood up and headed for the control panel.

Brad was still on stage, relishing his opportunity to taunt the band. He had moved on to his third victim and was now forcefully moving Alfie's eyelids up and down.

Out of nowhere the band stopped playing, and all the stage lights abruptly shut off. The curtains whipped shut, and Brad found himself alone in the darkness.

Unfazed by the dramatic change to his surroundings, he called out, "Hey, what happened?" The sliver of light at the bottom of the stage curtain was an inviting exit, but Brad had one last friend to greet.

He strolled over to Meaty, who was now in standing position, and squared up in front of the hulking gorilla. He leaned in close to the creature's face and looked into his cold, desolate eyes. "I'd jack you up," Brad whispered. He reached up and took the crown from Meaty's head and placed it on his own. Meaty's eyes darted to the side and looked directly and unmistakably at Brad. In an instant mix of shock and terror Brad stumbled backwards, falling down on the stage as the crown tumbled off his head. He pulled himself to his feet and was baffled when he saw that Meaty's eyes were back to looking straight ahead.

Brad backed up, not wanting to take his eyes off the creature as he felt behind for an opening in the curtain. He ducked out quickly and emerged on the other side to see his three friends still sitting at the table. Brad threw his hands up, "It's official. I'm done." He hopped off stage, trying to pull it together.

All of a sudden the digital countdown clock high above surged back on, although the power remained off on the rest of the stage. This time instead of white, the numbers were glowing red—and the countdown began.

Sixty minutes. 59:59, 59:58, 59:57… but only Perry noticed. And he was way too messed up to figure out that something was not right.

Hometown Entrepreneur Still Missing

Silas Skaggs, owner of the popular arcade-pizzeria Marinara has not been found and the trail is going cold

It has been a little over two weeks since the disappearance of Mr. Skaggs, who was last seen at the grand opening of his hugely successful restaurant, Marinara. Since that day, only a few clues have surfaced as officials and the public try to solve this mystery.

The last person to see Silas Skaggs was his son, several hours after closing on Marinara's first day of business. "Out of the blue my father walked behind the building into an open field between us and the woods. I remember there was wind, and the wild grass was swaying against my chest. He stopped and turned around to look at me. 'My work here is done,' he said. We looked at one another, and he gave me a nod, then walked right into the trees."

Sheriffs have recently scoured the area of woods behind Marinara, but with so little evidence, they still don't have a tangible lead on the direction the man may have went. "We brought out the search dogs, and they couldn't even pick up a scent," Deputy Sheriff Roy Dean said. "It's like he vanished into thin air."

One of the only solid clues investigators have uncovered is a small notepad found inside the drawer of Mr. Skaggs' nightstand. Inside were reportedly graphic depictions of people on fire and crude sketches of nightmarish monsters. Only one sentence was found within the notepad, although it was obsessively scribbled many times throughout. It read: "Can a good deed redeem a bad one?"

Authorities are fairly confident the drawings of fire are related to a past traumatic experience. Silas Skaggs was the lone guard-on-duty during the fateful D-Block prison fire that killed over a hundred inmates decades ago. Authorities are not sure what the drawings of monsters represent at this time.

Currently, the missing man's son has stepped into the role of overseeing daily operations at the restaurant they opened together just a few short weeks ago. Asked if he felt overwhelmed by his new role, he responded, "I'm still the janitor. And until my father walks through that door, that's what I'll remain. I'll see to it his exact plans are carried out."

For now it seems Marinara is in good hands. The rumors and hearsay of its owner's disappearance have only fueled interest. Lines have been forming outside its door almost every night, keeping workers steady and busy until the hopeful return of the man who built it ground up.

CHAPTER TEN

Keaton and Chrissy had been searching hopelessly throughout Marinara for a hidden nook where they might be able to get a little bit of privacy. They eventually found their way to The Janitor's office, and for a moment Keaton thought that he'd struck gold. He reached out and turned the doorknob, but it appeared locked. In his hormone-driven desperation he twisted it back and forth a few more times, hoping that the unusually sturdy metal door would suddenly give, but it was not to be. Keaton kicked the bottom of the door, and the two moved on in their quest.

In the middle of arcade row, an intense rivalry was brewing at the Super Sprint racing arcade where Ben was challenging Perry for all the glory. Arcade row was a nickname bestowed by the employees of Marinara, and it was pretty much exactly what one would expect: two long rows of arcades facing each other with a walkway in-between.

Ben was used to simple joysticks and just couldn't master the janky steering wheel of Super Sprint, so naturally Perry decided that would be the game he would practice relentlessly on. Although Ben held most of the high scores on the floor,

Super Sprint was Perry's singular conquest, and he had a special way to prove it.

Perry held all the top ten scores on the game, but instead of putting his three letter initials, he'd decided to get creative and leave a message for any potential challenger. It read as follows:

EVE-RYO-NEK-NOW-STH-ATP-ERR-YIS-THE-MAN

Unfortunately for Perry, kids and close friends would aim not for the top score, but for the coveted tenth spot. MAN would be regularly changed to ASS, POO or FAT which would genuinely piss Perry off every time. It became an anonymous game of chess, and Perry spent more time maintaining the tenth score than any of the nine above it.

Ben had never beaten Perry at the game, but tonight they were in the midst of one of their closest and most epic showdowns yet. It was the second to last lap, and they were neck and neck. Sarah cheered as Ben's red block car edged past Perry's yellow one, bumping it out of the way as he narrowly took the lead.

The excitement caught Brad's attention, and he headed over to see what he was missing. He was holding an ice cream cone three scoops tall that was leaning precariously to one side. "Um... yummy!" he announced, attempting to deep throat the entire thing.

Ben was so zeroed in that he tuned out both Sarah's cheering and Brad's stupid comments. It was the last lap, and victory would at last be his.

Perry shot a hurried glance over his shoulder to Brad's

frozen treat. "Where did you get that?" he demanded, with the lethal eagerness of a plump child.

"Kitchen," Brad replied. "Back of the freezer."

Perry immediately let go of the steering wheel and made a beeline for the kitchen. His yellow car veered off, then smashed into the guardrail, flipped over and exploded. "Damn it Perry!" Ben shouted. A few seconds later Ben's car crossed the finish line in first place.

"Doesn't count!" Perry yelled back. Ben didn't give Perry the satisfaction of a rebuttal because he knew he wouldn't win the argument. All he could do was just stand there and silently fume while mentally giving his friend the finger.

Ben's despair was short lived as Keaton poked his head around the arcade and leaned in. "Hey. I think it's time," he said, wiggling his eyebrows. "You know a good spot?"

"Broom closet. It's to the left of the stage, opposite a staircase," Ben said with a subtle, congratulatory head nod.

"What's down the staircase?" Keaton asked.

"The basement, but it's freezing down there. I'd stick with the closet if I were you," Ben replied.

"Roger that," Keaton said loudly while aggressively patting Ben on the back. After waiting impatiently for so long, he was pumped to be getting things started with Chrissy but couldn't resist spinning the steering wheel one time. "Damn, I do love this game," Keaton said. "Okay, one race boys."

****

The countdown clock above the stage was reaching an end, and the bright red numbers flashed: 00:03, 00:02, 00:01, 00:00.

The speaker announced "It's Showtime!" to an empty dining pit, and the curtains, tables and floor lightly trembled.

****

After making Chrissy endure a few more than one race with the boys, Keaton led her into the dining pit where they continued their search for the private spot Ben had suggested. "Are you sure you heard him right?" Chrissy asked.

"Ben said there was a broom closet somewhere around here," Keaton said as they approached a darkened area to the left of the stage.

"This has to be it," Chrissy said, walking up to a secluded door. Keaton reached out for the loose-fitting doorknob and pushed it open.

In the middle of the tiny room was a single, low-hanging lightbulb that was dangling from a thin wire. Keaton pulled on a string hanging next to it. The cloudy, low watt bulb barely illuminated the space, but it was enough to see that they were surrounded by shelves full of cleaning supplies and various mops and brooms. It was clear they were at the right place.

Keaton wasted no time in pulling Chrissy towards him and hungrily kissing the girl he'd been waiting for all night. She reached out her leg to kick the door shut behind them as Keaton's hands wandered up and down her body. Chrissy hastily threw her arms above her head to remove her shirt, bumping her wrist against the hanging lightbulb as she did so. They slid down to the floor while continuing to make out, focused entirely on one another now that their long-awaited union had finally come to fruition.

The lightbulb slowly swung backwards and forwards, rhythmically throwing darkness and then light against the wall behind them. Darkness and then light, darkness and then—a face emerged out of the murky recesses behind the shelves. The dim glow gradually revealed duck-like features shrouded in the shadows. Two wide, white eyes stared forward, unmoving and unblinking. They were transfixed on the two teenagers entangled on the closet floor. The bulb slowed to a stop, and Polly's face faded into the hidden background.

Keaton reached around Chrissy's back to unsnap her bra. "Hold on," she said, moving his hands away from the clasp. She stood up and pulled her shirt back on before he even had time to grasp what was happening.

"Wait. What?" Keaton asked in disbelief.

"I told you a kiss. If you want some more, you're gonna have to come and get it," Chrissy teased. She swung open the door and darted out of the closet.

"Are you serious?" Keaton said. He stood in the door frame, feeling both exasperated and intrigued by this new turn of events. He didn't waste any more time thinking about it though—the hunt was on.

Keaton quickly caught up to Chrissy in the dining pit. "What are you doing?" he asked.

"I thought you were a ladies' man. Haven't you ever heard of foreplay?" she said.

"And just what did you have in mind?" he said, moving closer.

Chrissy leaned in and kissed him on the neck. "Oh, just a little game."

"Of?" he asked.

She whispered in his ear. "Hide… and… seek."

Keaton put his hands on Chrissy's waist and leaned back to take a good look at her. "How drunk are you?" he asked.

"Very much drunk," she replied. "Why, what's wrong? Are you afraid of a little chase?"

"You can have the whole building. I'll sniff you out in five minutes," Keaton said, as cool and self-assured as ever.

"Then you'll get the prize," Chrissy said.

"So what do I count to?" Keaton asked.

"Count to… sixty-nine," Chrissy said with a coy smirk.

Keaton placed his hands over his eyes and began. "One, one thousand; two, one thousand…"

"No, you'll peek!" Chrissy said. "Back to the closet till you're done." She walked him back into the broom closet, then grabbed Keaton by his shirt and pulled him in for a long, hard kiss. "Don't take forever," she said as she pulled away and closed the door behind her. "And no peeking!"

Keaton was left in the dark. He started counting once again and barely got to twelve one thousand before growing impatient. He reached above his head and turned the light on, squinting against the sudden brightness. "Twenty-seven, one thousand; forty-three, one thousand…" he blurted out randomly.

In the distance he heard a faint pitter patter of footsteps descending the staircase that led to the basement. "Oh, I'm on to you now," Keaton said. He opened the closet door and headed towards the sound.

At the top of the steps Keaton flipped on a switch that lit up the stairwell. He tiptoed down the steep, narrow flight encased by concrete walls and could actually feel the temperature getting colder just as Ben had said. When he reached the bottom, Keaton gingerly placed his ear up against a thin, simple door. He heard a light scurrying inside and smiled to himself. He'd got her.

Keaton flung open the door, expecting to surprise Chrissy on the other side, but it was too dark to see anything. He ran his hand up and down the wall but couldn't seem to find the light switch, so he reached into his back pocket and pulled out a lighter. He casually flipped it open and struck a flame as the door closed behind him. Keaton stepped cautiously to avoid tripping as the small flame could only muster enough light to reveal a few feet of space at a time.

He slowly explored until he had a rough layout of the room. It was a large, open space with metal shelves lining the walls containing everything from old paint cans to spare bricks. There were large crates full of dry foods stacked aimlessly about, and everything was covered in so much dust it seemed like the room had been long forgotten. "Chrissy, you're busted. Turn on the lights," he called out.

Keaton was startled by a high-pitched, cartoonish sounding giggle, and he spun around to the direction it came from. "That's pretty good. Wasn't expecting the creepy laugh," he said.

He spotted a pink scarf peeking out from behind a couple large stacks of crates. As he walked towards it, the scarf inched back behind them. "Ah, there you are," he said. Keaton moved in closer and held the lighter in front of his face to better see what was between them.

There was nothing there. No Chrissy. Not even the pink scarf. Keaton could feel his heart beating. He was suddenly aware of just how dark and isolated the room was. How thick and soundproof the concrete walls were. And something didn't feel right about him staying down there for a minute longer.

"Chrissy? Come out," he said, knowing in his gut that she wasn't listening.

A light puff of breath came from seemingly nowhere, and the flickering flame of his lighter was blown out. Another giggle came from behind the stacks of crates.

Keaton tried fervently to reignite the flame, sparking the lighter over and over again until it finally caught. He turned to the crates and exhaled with relief when he saw nothing. "Man, for a second there I thought—" Polly blasted through the crates headfirst, her eyes wide open with madness. Her fully outstretched arms violently struck Keaton to the ground. His horrified scream fell on deaf ears.

****

Chrissy was crouched down between a trio of arcade games where she'd been hiding ever since leaving Keaton in the broom closet. Her legs were getting tired, and she was growing bored. She peeked out one last time and sighed in exasperation when Keaton was still nowhere in sight.

She squeezed out from between the machines and stood up to look around the game floor. "Keaton!" she called out, but there was no reply. She marched down to the dining pit, calling his name again, only to be met with more silence. Chrissy walked over to the broom closet and pulled open the door, half expecting to find Keaton passed out inside. But it was empty. Then the light of the basement staircase caught her attention. *That wasn't on before*, she thought.

Chrissy stomped down the stairs, annoyed that she was supposed to be the hider and now had to be the seeker. She opened the door at the bottom of the staircase and fumbled around for the light switch but couldn't find one. It was cold and eerily quiet, and she wanted out as soon as possible. "Keaton. Are you in here?" Chrissy called out from the doorway. She grew more anxious with each passing second, and the pitch black wasn't easing her nerves. "Okay, this isn't funny. If you don't answer me I'm going to get help."

She waited a few moments before accepting she wasn't getting a response and then clamored back up the steps, half in anger, half from a feeling of dread that had rooted itself deep in the pit of her stomach.

CHAPTER ELEVEN

Inside the kitchen the rest of the group had convened for an ice cream break. Perry had a cone in each hand and lifted one as an offering when Chrissy came bursting through the flapping door. "No thanks," Chrissy said before getting straight to the point. "Have any of you seen Keaton?"

"No, I thought you were together," Ben said.

"We were playing hide and seek. I think he might be passed out in the basement," Chrissy said with a rush of concern in her voice.

"Now why would you think that?" Brad asked dismissively, licking his fingers after chomping down the last of his cone.

"Because the staircase light was on *Brad*. I walked down to the door, but it was dark and I couldn't find the switch," she said.

"It's overhead and to the left," Ben said. "I have no idea why those morons put it there."

"Would you guys come with me?" Chrissy asked. "If he's passed out, I'm gonna need some help."

"Of course we will," Sarah replied.

Perry plopped off the counter. "Lightweight."

****

The group reached the basement staircase and began walking down single file with Ben leading the way. Halfway down they heard what sounded like a sharp gasp and the rubber soles of sneakers frantically scuffing against concrete. It was immediately followed by a penetrating, shrill giggle from the other side of the door. "He he he!"

Ben instinctively stopped to process what he'd just heard. Everyone stood still, concentrating as they anticipated the next sound. "Did you hear that?" Ben whispered to Brad.

"Yeah," Brad replied, a hint of unease registering on his face. "What the hell was it?"

Ben was rattled but responded with the only reasonable thing it could be. "Probably just Keaton messing around," he said with feigned confidence. Ben then continued down the steps as an uncontrollable shiver ran down his spine. Everyone else followed suit, but their posture had become tense and their steps hesitant.

They all huddled at the base of the stairs, squeezing tightly against the thin door. Reluctant as he was, Ben knew he had no other choice and reached out for the handle. Out of the silence, another giggle echoed horrifically throughout the space on the other side. This time it was louder and different than the one before, almost more of a demented cackle. Whatever was in there was inviting them to enter.

Everyone exchanged alarmed glances, not wanting to know what could have possibly made that terrifying sound. Not wanting to know what lay in wait behind the deceptive safety of that thin door.

Brad suddenly sprung into action and pushed Ben forward. "Go! Go!" he shouted. In what was more a reaction than a conscious choice, Ben threw the door wide open. The boys burst into the dark, cavernous room, crossing the threshold in a flurry of testosterone and fear. The girls followed right behind them, equally as courageous but not nearly as gung ho. Ben reached overhead to his left, and when the lights came on, the blood drained from every last one of their faces.

In the center of the room Polly was straddling Keaton's twitching body. She jerked her head up, wild-eyed and crazed like a startled animal. Her pink scarf was tied tightly around Keaton's neck, crushing his airway as she used it to strangle him. His face had turned an unnatural shade of purple, and his veins were bulging out like a colony of worms had embedded themselves under his skin. Keaton's eyes were nearly popping out of his skull, and they turned in desperation towards his friends, pleading wordlessly for help.

For the briefest of seconds the room froze in time, as if the moment were a still frame from a horror film somebody had hit pause on. Everyone stared in paralyzed disbelief, trying to wrap their minds around the impossibly surreal scene that lay before them. Brad looked at his friend on the floor and was the first to break out of the daze. "Get off him!" he screamed, rushing towards the monster with all the fury of a soldier running into battle. With everything he had, Brad kicked Polly square under the chin, knocking her backwards off Keaton and onto the concrete floor. Brad screamed as a jolt of pain ripped through him, and he fell to the floor clenching his foot.

Seeing Polly on the ground, Ben ran over and pulled hard on one of the tall metal shelves. It crashed down on her with a deafening sound and an avalanche of debris and dust. The animatronic lay motionless under the weight of the wreckage, her eyes closed shut.

Ben dropped to a knee by next to Perry who was already trying to untie the scarf knotted around Keaton's neck. "Hurry, get it off!" Ben shouted, his panicked words lost amongst the other shouts and screams of everyone surrounding him.

"I'm trying!" Perry said as his trembling fingers pried in vain at the knot. "I can't get it!"

Brad pulled out his pocket knife and yelled out to Ben. He slid it across the floor, and Ben quickly removed the scarf with a couple of carefully placed cuts. Ben slipped the knife into his pocket as Perry hopelessly shook Keaton's shoulders.

Sarah knelt down alongside the boys. "Get out of the way," she said assertively. She leaned down and put her ear against Keaton's mouth while placing her fingers on the inside of his wrist. "He doesn't have a pulse."

Sarah positioned herself over Keaton and began to perform CPR. After completing several cycles, she stopped and checked his vitals again. Keaton's body was still as the group held their collective breath. Sarah strained her senses and waited what felt like an eternity for any sign of life. As much as she willed it though, she could feel neither a breath nor a heartbeat and looked up at her friends with tears welling in her eyes.

"Is he…" Brad asked, trailing off as he found himself unable to say the word.

Sarah simply nodded as the tears streamed down her cheeks.

Chrissy let out a gut-wrenching scream and began wailing uncontrollably. She threw herself onto the ground beside Keaton and wrapped her arms around him. She cried out his name as she grasped at his face, trying to shake him back into existence. Sarah reached over to comfort her friend, and Chrissy crumbled into her arms. "Somebody wake me up. Somebody wake me up. Somebody please—" Chrissy's eyes rolled back, and her head fell to the side as she passed out.

"Chrissy," Sarah said, trying to coax her to awaken. "Chrissy!" But she was out cold. The stillness was shattered by the piercing sound of metal colliding with concrete which boomed from behind them. A dust cloud quickly flooded the air, and the boys jumped blindly to their feet.

The fallen shelf had been launched to the other side of the room, and Polly was nowhere to be seen. But she was somewhere to be heard. The sinister cackle bounced off the walls, seeming to come from everywhere and nowhere all at once. "He he he he he…"

Sarah laid Chrissy down and shot to her feet as fast as she could. "Where is it?" she shouted, feeling her heart begin to tighten. Everyone scanned the room, but nobody thought to look at the floor, so they didn't notice the pair of snow-white eyes appear out of the darkness. Two giant hands shot out and grabbed Sarah by the ankles.

Before Sarah could even look down, Polly jerked her feet out from under her, and she fell headfirst with a hollow thud against the cold, hard concrete. Polly fully emerged from the shadows and reached down to pick Sarah up as if she weighed nothing. She hurled her across the room into a metal scaffold, and Sarah fell to the ground unmoving.

Seeing Sarah in jeopardy made something in Ben's mind snap. It took him to the place where logic and the instinct for self-preservation are overcome by the brave and undeniably selfless need to protect. He let out an enraged scream and charged full speed towards Polly, tackling her with a strength he didn't know he had. They struggled on the ground with both trying to gain the advantage, but the realization was quickly setting in that Ben had simply caught Polly off guard and that soon he would be completely overtaken.

Brad looked on helplessly as Polly and Ben rolled around in a tangle of limbs. He anxiously surveyed the room for something to use until he spotted a weathered handicap parking sign in a corner. It wasn't the sign he was after though, but the metal pole connected to it. He grabbed the pole and easily kicked off the rusted sign, then cocked it above his shoulder waiting for an opening to strike.

Perry was standing just a few feet away in an almost trance-like state. Brad whipped around to face him. "Grab something man!" he yelled out.

Perry glanced down at Ben and Polly on the floor with a detached, blank expression. His eyes slowly moved over to Keaton's lifeless body. It was the last thing in the world he wanted to look at, but he couldn't look away. Perry suddenly took off in a sprint straight out of the room and up the stairs.

"Perry!" Brad called out, shaking his head in disgust at his friend's cowardice.

Polly was now straddling Ben with her hands tightly around his throat as he flailed violently, trying to escape. Brad crept up behind her, lifting the pole into attack position. While still restraining Ben, Polly methodically turned her head a full

180 degrees to look directly at Brad. The ghastly, unnatural movement dropped Brad's jaw. "My God," he said faintly, the words barely touching his lips. Her head then swiveled back around to focus on finishing off Ben.

"Stay down!" Brad yelled as he reared back. Ben caught on to the plan and, mustering all his strength, pushed Polly's head up as far as he possibly could. Brad smashed the pole into the back of her skull with full force, and she immediately fell limp on top of Ben. Brad's adrenaline redlined and he cocked the pole back one more time as he let out a primal scream. In one fluid motion, Polly leapt up from the ground, grabbing Brad by the neck in mid-air and ferociously smashing him into the concrete. As Brad languished in pain, Polly snatched her scarf off the floor and turned back to Ben with a vengeance.

Ben was now sitting upright but still gasping for breath when he saw Polly stalking towards him. Without the time or strength to stand, Ben scooted backwards as fast as he could— but her stride was long, and she easily caught up to him. She wrapped the scarf tightly around his neck and dragged him across the floor as he pulled and tugged at the suffocating knot. Polly sunk down to the floor and leaned up against a stack of wooden crates. She effortlessly manhandled Ben into a sitting position between her splayed legs, choking him from behind as the scarf pulled his head back against hers.

Brad climbed back to his feet and grabbed the metal pole. As he approached, he quickly realized that Polly was using Ben as a shield while simultaneously draining the life out of him— it was the physical manifestation of killing two stones with one bird.

Brad was aiming for an open shot to her head, but there

was no way he was getting one, especially with the long, unwieldy pole as his weapon. And Ben was running out of time. In a last-ditch bid for any sort of assault, Brad called out, "Move your legs!"

Ben pulled in his legs and Brad unleashed on Polly's, smashing the pole into her mechanical appendages over and over. Brad pulverized her legs, splintering off metal fragments everywhere. But it was no use. Polly didn't budge; she didn't even flinch. She either didn't feel pain or, the more frightening alternative, *she did*.

Brad could see that Ben was beginning to lose consciousness, and he was confronted with the possibility that all hope was lost—he was going to have to watch his friend die. Just as Ben's eyelids flickered closed, Perry burst through the basement door, wielding an ax like a deranged madman and sprinting full speed towards Polly with an enraged battle cry.

"Get down!" Perry screamed, and Ben was instantly pulled back from the precipice of oblivion. He mustered what little strength was left in his battered body and bent his neck down as far as he possibly could, curling his chin tightly against his chest. It was a perilously small window for error, but Perry took his only chance and swung the ax through the air. The blade sliced clear through Polly's neck and wedged itself into the crate behind her, leaving her severed head balanced precariously on the blade itself. Her eyes were wide open, frozen straight ahead in a crazed death mask. A thin stream of dark brown liquid slowly trickled out of her neck and down the ax blade.

With some assistance from Brad and Perry, Ben shakily stood. "Thank you," he said, meaning it in more ways than one. After getting his bearings, he quickly rushed over to Sarah's side. Ben shook her gently, rousing her awake. "Hey, it's me," he said, delicately taking her hand in his. "Can you stand?"

Sarah nodded and he helped her up.

Brad and Perry were tending to Chrissy who was conscious but disoriented and in shock. They got her to a half-standing position, but as soon as she saw Keaton, she struggled free and fell to her knees by his side. Brad tenderly placed a hand on her shoulder. "He's gone Chrissy."

"I'm not leaving him," she sobbed, stroking his cheek with the back of her hand as if he were simply sleeping.

Ben looked on with a heavy heart, but he knew he had to get Chrissy and everyone else out of the building as soon as possible. He reached into his pocket and pulled out what was once the coveted silver key. "Here," he said as he handed it to Brad. "You guys get the front door open. I'll get her out of here." Brad nodded and clenched a protective fist around the key.

Ben lowered himself beside Chrissy and looked up at Sarah, Brad and Perry who each seemed to have a different emotion drawn across their face. "You guys go. We'll be right behind you," he told them.

"I'm staying with you," Sarah said, but Ben shook his head.

He looked at her firmly, letting her know without words he was steadfast in his decision. "No, go with the guys and get the hell out of here. I'll be right behind you," he said.

The trio remained still. They knew they couldn't stay down there, but as afraid as they had been to enter the room, they were twice as afraid to leave it. There was only one question on all their minds—was there something even more insidious lying in wait?

"Go!" Ben shouted. There was no more time for second guessing. His eyes connected with Perry's and then with Brad's. "Take care of her," he said.

The three took off running up the stairs, with Brad taking the lead, Perry in the back and Sarah between them. Ben watched as they ran out of sight, then turned his attention to Chrissy and put a reassuring arm around her.

She gazed down at the boy who had won her heart and held his still warm hand. "I can't leave him," she said. "I can't."

"I know. I don't want to either," Ben said. But he also knew they had no choice. "We'll come back for him once it's safe. I promise."

Chrissy's breathing had slowed to a normal pace, and the stream of tears had dried around her sad, weary eyes.

"He was just here," she said. And those simple words brought Ben's racing mind to a screeching halt. The finality was almost too much to grasp, but it now sunk in that he was never going to see his friend again.

Chrissy leaned into Ben's embrace.

"He was just here…" she said.

CHAPTER TWELVE

The front door to Marinara was like a beacon of salvation after a hurricane at sea. It felt like that anyway to Brad, Sarah and Perry who had all just breathlessly arrived there after a rabid sprint from the basement. The door was made of clear, lightly tinted glass, and inside the windowless building, it was the only reminder that the safety of the outside world lay just inches away.

Brad hurriedly slid in the ornate, silver key Ben had given him—but it wouldn't turn.

He tried flipping the key upside down and shoved it in as far as it would go, but it became frighteningly obvious that it was not going to unlock the door in front of them. "I don't know why it's not working!" Brad said.

Perry shot a nervous glance over his shoulder, half expecting a set of razor-sharp claws to rip into his flesh at any second. "Try it again!" he insisted.

Brad made one last attempt, but again he was unsuccessful. They all soon realized that they would have to find another way.

****

The countdown clock over the stage was ticking dangerously close to zero again as the red numbers flashed their final warning: 00:03, 00:02, 00:01, 00:00. The speaker crackled to life, but the usual voice that rang out was disturbingly cheerful—almost foreboding in its exuberance. "It's showtime!"

****

Sarah heard the distant announcement and felt her blood run cold. "We have to get out of here. I think something bad is about to happen."

"The hell with this," Brad said, shoving the key in his pocket. He picked up the metal pole he had carried from the basement. "Stand back," he instructed. Brad hit the pole full force against the glass door, but it simply bounced off, leaving the door completely and unbelievably unscathed. Puzzled, Brad swung one more time. Not even a scratch.

His eyes darted around for anything he could use as a battering ram. Perry pointed to a metal token dispenser a few feet away. It was heavy, but the two managed to lift it up. They backed up a good ten feet from the door and took a few deep breaths to get themselves pumped. "On the count of three," Brad said.

He counted down, and they sprinted towards the door at full speed. With all their mass and momentum, they smashed the coin dispenser into the glass pane—and were stopped dead in their tracks.

The three looked at the door in disbelief. "What's happening?" Perry said. But none of them wanted to say out loud the thing they all feared. They couldn't admit the reality nobody would be able to accept. They were trapped.

****

Ben's reassuring words had calmed Chrissy down, and he saw his opening for them to leave. "C'mon, let's get out of here," he said. Ben put his arm around Chrissy and helped her to her feet. They walked over to the basement door, but just as Ben reached for the handle, Chrissy grabbed his hand away. Her eyes were alive and alert, her ear tilted towards the stairwell.

"There's something up there," she whispered. They both stood in silence, listening for whatever it was.

"I don't hear anything," Ben said. "Come on, they're waiting on us."

"No!" she said adamantly, holding tightly to his arm. Every instinct in her body told her not to go up those stairs.

Ben could tell that whatever Chrissy *thought* she heard, she was taking it very seriously. "We have to go up some time," he said gently. "I'll go take a look and make sure it's okay."

Chrissy was trembling, frantically shaking her head not to do it. Ben listened at the door one more time and still didn't hear a thing. He tentatively reached for the handle.

Just as he was about to open the door, Chrissy yanked him back and flicked off the basement light. A split second later a deep thud echoed down the stairwell. Something heavy had set foot on top of the steps. Something heavier than Brad, Perry, Sarah—or maybe all three of them put together. The stairs creaked and groaned as it walked down.

Ben grabbed Chrissy's hand and pulled her into the shadows. It all happened so fast that he didn't even notice the stockpile of wooden beams leaning against the wall, and he came within a splinter of sending the whole thing tumbling down. He leaned his head back and exhaled, cursing himself for being so reckless.

"Ben," Chrissy's voice trembled.

"Shh, quiet," he whispered. "Run when I say."

Ben realized that Chrissy's fingernails were digging so hard into his hand that they were cutting through his flesh, but he didn't loosen his grip.

Chrissy began to panic. She tried her best to control the soft whimpering, but as the footsteps grew louder, so did she. It had to be close. Maybe right on the other side of the door by now. Then the footsteps stopped.

Ben whispered a plea in Chrissy's ear as softly as he possibly could. "Shh, it'll hear you." Chrissy grit her teeth, trying to mute the earsplitting sound of her own breathing.

The basement door creaked open, and faint light spilled into the dark room. A bulky silhouette stepped down onto the floor. The outline moving slightly against the darkness was so terrifying that it took all of Chrissy's willpower not to scream. But she knew staying undetected was their only chance. The difference between living and dying was as fragile as a single audible sound.

Ben pressed his hand tightly over Chrissy's mouth to smother any noises that might escape. A bead of sweat trickled down his forehead, and he squinted at the stinging sensation as the salty liquid reached his eye. But Ben didn't move a muscle.

Gus' long, rodent-like tail swooped back and forth in the air like a serpent seeking its prey. The giant possum had shed his straw hat and banjo, and it was striking how much more threatening he looked without those simple objects. Ben and Chrissy pressed their backs even more tightly against the wall, imploring the deep shadows of the basement to conceal them from the beast.

Gus walked to the center of the room. His head was long, practically made up of all snout and mouth. Countless sharp, little white teeth lined his jaws. His beady, pink eyes moved slowly over the basement then stopped on the stockpile of wooden beams. Chrissy's eyes quivered as tears flowed over Ben's hand.

Gus turned his whole body towards the two and paused. Ben was sure that Gus was looking straight into his eyes, and he had to fight the overwhelming instinct to flee. Ben made up his mind right then and there. If Gus took one step towards them, they were going to make a run for it. But out of nowhere, Gus abruptly turned and began walking away from them. He stopped in front of Polly and looked down at her decapitated corpse. He tilted his head like a curious animal, staring at hers which still rested on the ax blade.

Ben seized the moment and yelled "Go!" The two bolted for the staircase, not looking back. If they had, they would have seen Gus so fixated on Polly that he didn't even acknowledge or seem to care about their fleeing. But he didn't need to. They weren't getting far.

****

Sarah sighed with relief as Ben and Chrissy came running up from the basement, but it was short lived when she saw the looks they both had on their faces.

"Is it open?" Ben said as he grabbed the door handle, only to find it still locked firmly in place.

"The key won't work," Brad said. "We can't get out."

"Give it to me," Ben said, and Brad handed him the silver key.

"I'm telling you, it doesn't work," Brad said as Ben slid it into the slot.

Ben had to find out firsthand what his friend was trying to tell him. "I don't understand—this is the key!" he bellowed.

"Hurry," Chrissy cried out.

Ben looked around in desperation, as Brad had done only minutes before. His eyes settled on the metal pole.

"You're wasting your time man," Brad said. "I already tried it."

"What in the hell," Ben said.

"Is it made out of some kind of special glass or something?" Sarah asked.

"No way," Ben replied. "Those cheap-asses would never spring for something like that."

"Should we try to take off the hinges?" Perry said.

"No time," Ben said. "We have to leave now."

"I don't know; that might work," Brad said.

Ben turned swiftly to Brad. "You don't understand. There's another one. It was in the basement."

"Oh God," Sarah said.

"Ben, isn't there a back door?" Perry asked.

"Yeah, but we'd have to go past the basement and stage to get to it," Ben said.

"Where's the nearest phone?" Sarah asked.

****

Gus had not moved an inch since Ben and Chrissy escaped from the basement. He stood over Polly's mangled and contorted body, completely motionless save for the rhythmic swaying of his tail. He leaned in, almost meeting Polly eye to eye, then swiped her head off the ax blade. Gus gripped the handle and effortlessly pulled the ax out from the wooden crate it was wedged into.

He turned away from Polly and began walking towards the stairwell, dragging the ax behind him as he went. The blade scraping against the concrete sent sparks flying into the air, and the harsh sound ricocheted off the basement walls. Gus lumbered up the staircase with the ax lazily clunking over each stair behind him. The hunt had begun.

****

Ben led the group to the employee break room, and they flooded through its door, softly but assuredly closing it behind them. Brad immediately noticed a tall set of metal lockers not far from the entrance. He put his back against them, but they were unyielding. "Here, help me move this," he grunted. Perry and Ben quickly lent a hand, and the three slid it in front of the door.

Brad looked to Sarah and Chrissy. "Could you two hang here and listen for anything coming?" They both responded with a nod, and Brad headed over to the break room cabinets.

"What are you looking for?" Perry asked as Brad rifled through the cupboards and drawers.

"Weapons. Anything we can use," Brad replied. "Help me."

Perry joined in, and the two of them turned the place inside out.

Ben remembered the whole reason they were in the break room and rushed over to the telephone. He picked up the receiver, but there was no dial tone, only dead air. He pushed the switch hook down repeatedly but to no avail. Ben was now more perplexed than worried, but that would soon change.

With the receiver still against his ear, Ben began to hear what sounded like breathing on the other end of the line.

"Hello? Is anybody there?" Ben asked cautiously.

A few seconds of silence passed. Then a muffled, distorted voice repeated back to him slowly: *Hello? Is anybody there?*

Ben furrowed his brow in confusion. He pressed the receiver tightly against his ear and again heard the heavy breathing. Static mixed with electric pops invaded the line then gradually gave way to the faint sound of a faraway voice. It was a female voice, and it sounded like it was transmitting through a crude radio from a distant, otherworldly place. She sounded around Ben's age. Her voice was urgent, clearly gripped with fear. *If anyone can hear this, we're trapped. We can't stop them. Please. We need help.*

"Who is this? Hello?" Ben said. "Can you hear me? Hello?" But the line went dead. Ben's unsteady hand placed the receiver back on its hook.

"What is it?" Sarah asked.

"I'm not sure," Ben said, choosing his words carefully. He didn't want to freak everyone out even more than they already were. "It sounded like a girl. She said she was trapped. Then it went dead."

The reactions on everyone's faces told him that he had not succeeded in his goal.

They were all reaching in their minds for any halfway rational explanation that might explain what Ben had just said. But there wasn't one. They all knew that as much as they wished this wasn't real, it was, and there was no denying it.

"So what are we going to do?" Perry asked, chewing nervously on a fingernail.

"Well, there's nothing in here," Brad said, surrounded by open cabinets. "All we've got is this one shitty pole between all of us. We need to find weapons."

Perry gestured to the barricaded door. "And where are we going to get them? Out there?"

Brad quickly countered. "As of right now we're trapped in this building, and we can't get ahold of the outside world. That *thing* out there is looking for us, and it's going to find us sooner or later. Then what?"

No one spoke. Everyone was searching for their own answer to the dilemma.

"There are all kinds of tools and stuff in the maintenance room," Ben suggested.

Perry locked eyes with his friend. "You cannot be serious."

"Brad's right," Ben said. "We're sitting ducks if we stay here. We have to chance it."

Tears were welling in Chrissy's eyes. "I can't. I can't go back out there," she said, backing away from the door like a frightened child.

"Ben, that's suicide man. I really think we should hide," Perry said.

"And I do too," Ben said. "But we have to be able to defend ourselves."

"If that bastard walks up on me, I'm taking him down," Brad said, his words charged with conviction. "I'm not waiting to die."

"So we'll get weapons, then hide and figure a way out of here," Ben said. He met Sarah's eyes to make sure she was still with him.

"Okay, let's go," Brad urged.

"No," Perry said, as somber and resolute as anyone in that room had ever seen him. He glanced over to Chrissy who was clearly still shaken. "We're gonna hide and wait this out."

"We need to stick together," Ben said.

Perry and Ben looked right at one another, the two best friends silently imploring the other to agree. They had been through a lot of life together and had each other's backs the entire time, but this was different. This was the biggest decision either one of them ever had to make. And neither one of them budged.

Chrissy turned to Sarah and grasped her hand. "Stay with us," she pleaded.

"I'm sorry," Sarah said as her eyes filled with tears.

Neither of the girls tried to change the other's mind—they respected and understood the reasonings. They just hugged each other longer and tighter than ever before.

Ben was forced to accept that Perry and Chrissy weren't coming along and had no choice but to move forward. "So are you two staying in here?" he asked.

Perry glanced around the barren room. "There's nowhere to hide."

"Then where?" Ben asked.

"I think the kitchen," Perry said. "There are plenty of spaces, and it's close."

"Okay," Ben said with a nod. "We'll meet you there once we find what we need."

Nobody in that room *wanted* to split up. But the time had come. Everyone in the two groups shared embraces and words of love.

"Be careful Benjamin Franklin," Perry said.

Ben cracked a smile. "You too."

Perry looked over to Chrissy. "You ready?" he asked. Chrissy nodded.

The group listened intently at the door but heard nothing. The boys quickly pushed the lockers out of the way, and Ben cracked the door open to peer outside. Everything seemed to be still and quiet. A little too still and quiet for comfort. It would have *almost* been better if they had seen one of the creatures because at least they'd know where the enemy stood.

Ben couldn't help but take one last look behind him at his friends. As much as he didn't want to acknowledge it, he knew deep down that it might be the last time he ever saw them.

"Let's go," Ben whispered.

They snuck out, one by one, through the door and away from the relative yet temporary safety of their hiding spot.

The group was now divided and would take different paths. But the goal was steadfastly the same for all—get out alive.

Radio Silence...

Late last night, widespread TV and radio blackouts occurred in conjunction with strange interference

During a rerun of M*A*S*H, Sandy Cunningham walloped her television set so hard that it almost fell off its stand. She was used to the two long antennas spoiling a climactic scene or going to complete static every now and then — but never like this. From about 10pm to 1am yesterday evening, throngs of folks around town reported TVs and radios dropping programming. But why it happened wasn't nearly as perplexing as what came on during the event.

Amongst the black and white static of their TVs, viewers were said to have seen random images of a horror movie fade in and out of the screen. Others saw snippets of what could be best described as a live-action children's program. Many of the distorted images were disturbing to say the least according to those watching. The likely explanation is that the TV sets picked up faint signals from far away broadcasts. But at the time of printing, no local or neighboring listings were found to have had either type of programming on during that time.

Radio listeners also experienced some unusual side-effects of the blackout. All channels were thick with static and interference, but every now and again some said a peculiar high pitch would break in, if only for a few seconds. More than one person interviewed said it resembled a human scream.

Renowned physicist Anthony Ericsson threw in his two cents regarding the matter. "Electromagnetic waves, like those used in our radios and TV sets, can be easily manipulated. They can be absorbed by something as simple as tin foil all the way up to a black hole — which clearly isn't the case here. I can sit here and throw a bunch of big words at you and theories, but in all honesty I simply don't know what caused it." Ericsson left the interview with a bit of wisdom. "As a scientist there's an old Hamlet line that I'm particularly fond of. It says there are more things in Heaven and Earth than are dreamt of in your philosophy."

On the more colorful side of things, local disc jockey Big Rod was working when he experienced the anomaly. During his popular segment, Big Rod's Rancid Rock Block, he received a call from a concerned listener. "I was spinning The Doors' 'Break on Through' when this chick called me from a McDonalds and asked where the hell the music went," Rod said. "That's when it hit me something was very wrong." Asked if he had ever encountered anything like the blackout before, Big Rod said, "[expletive] no, lady. That creepy [expletive] gave me the [expletive] creeps."

Reps from TV and radio stations have vowed to get to the bottom of the incident while assuring the public it won't happen again. For the sake of everybody working for the weekend — let's hope they are right.

CHAPTER THIRTEEN

Gus stood shrouded in a dark corner of the building, at ease in his nocturnal element. The ax was still gripped firmly in his hand, the blade resting against the carpet. His tail eagerly tapped against the floor, unable to contain its anticipation of the revelry that lay ahead.

A door opening nearby drew Gus' attention, and he turned his head to see the group filing out of the break room. But Gus remained hunched against the wall, biding his time as he savored a few more moments in the shadows.

****

The countertop island in the center of the kitchen still had flour scattered about and other remnants of the cooking that had been done there what seemed like a lifetime ago. Perry and Chrissy raced into the room, their eyes immediately darting around as they looked for somewhere to hide.

The island contained the large oven on one side and a considerable storage area on the other that was covered by a sliding metal door. Directly across from the oven was the steel fridge and a smaller stovetop oven, on top of which still sat the huge, two-foot tall vat of marinara. Other than those options, every spot in the room was too small to fit anything larger than a child.

The pair quickly assessed their options and decided on the storage area underneath the island. Perry slid back the metal door, and it recessed into the island's facade. The space inside was not nearly as large as it appeared from the outside. There was only enough room for one of them, and even then it would be pretty tight. "You stay here, I'll find somewhere else," Perry said.

Chrissy looked fondly at him, touched by his selflessness. She crawled into the space and pulled her knees against her chest. As Perry slid the door shut, Chrissy could feel the separation anxiety wash over her. It was pitch black inside, and she was now completely alone for the first time.

Perry wasted no time hesitating. He'd already thought of a backup plan just in case the first one didn't work out. He hurried over to the other side of the countertop island and opened the large oven. He hastily pulled out the racks and looked around for a place to stash them so as not to give away his location. He turned to the big fridge behind him and began stuffing the racks inside. They were awkward to maneuver, but he eventually worked them in and managed to shut the door. He opened the barren oven and climbed inside. There was nothing to do now but wait.

For a while the kitchen was completely still and silent, save for the buzzing of the fluorescent lights above which cast a cold, white light over the space. Out of nowhere a pair of beady, pink eyes appeared in the window of the kitchen's flapping door. Gus slowly scanned the room from one side to the other, panting rapidly like a starved animal.

The door opened with a creak so dreadful and drawn out that it was hard to tell if he was trying to be discreet or as torturous as possible. Gus paused in the doorway, taking in the layout of his new playground. Inside their confined spaces, both Perry and Chrissy's ears jolted towards the sound. They knew in an instant that *he* had arrived.

Gus walked into the room, leisurely surveying everything as he passed by. Through the oven's tinted window Perry could see a long, gnarly tail slithering past with an ax dragging alongside it. He held his breath, praying the monster wouldn't look below and find him there, helpless and completely vulnerable. Gus continued walking by the countertop island and made his way to the end of the kitchen as Perry exhaled and crumpled back against the rear of the oven.

The back wall was lined with stainless steel cupboards. Gus scraped his metal claws across the row as he walked past. It sounded like rusty nails tearing across a chalkboard, only twice as loud and piercing. Chrissy's hiding spot was like an echo chamber with four unforgiving metal walls callously ricocheting everything back at one another. She slammed her hands against her ears as the relentless barrage dug into her brain. Without realizing it Chrissy started to breathe in short gasps, and a rush of claustrophobia overcame her. She wanted so desperately to scream and burst out of her confinement, but she knew what would happen if she did. Chrissy tried to inhale a deep breath to calm herself, but the air felt heavy and stale, and it suddenly seemed like there wasn't enough of it within the small space. Her shallow breathing soon escalated into full-on hyperventilating.

A feeling of lightheadedness fell over her as a faint, high-pitched tone began to reverberate in her ears. The slow loss of consciousness took her to another place, a familiar place. A safe place where Chrissy thought of her mom and how every night she still came into her room to tuck her in, even though she was all grown up now. If there was any place in the whole wide world she could be at that moment, it would be in her warm bed with her mom kissing her on the forehead.

In a flash of light and screeching noise, an ax blade ripped through her reverie and the cupboard's metal door. Through the opening Chrissy could see Gus' face directly in front of her. His eyes were lifeless, and his jaw hung wide open as if it were unhinged. A hand blasted through the hole and grasped blindly for her. She let out a blood-curdling scream while trying to evade the thrashing claws.

Chrissy eluded Gus long enough that he withdrew his arm through the hole. As she took her first breath in what seemed like minutes, Gus ripped off the metal door and grabbed her by the hair, dragging her out into the brightness of the kitchen.

Gus pulled Chrissy up to a standing position and launched her over the countertop like she was a fraction of her size. She smashed through the overhanging pots and pans and slammed into the fridge across the room, slumping to the ground in a tangle of limbs. Gus looked down at her with merciless indifference as he walked around the island and laid his ax against the wall. He turned the palm of his hand upwards to inspect it, and Chrissy watched in horror as she saw that his fingers had chunks of her hair strung between them.

Chrissy stumbled to her feet, but a heavy kick to the gut from Gus knocked the wind out of her. She dropped to the floor, clutching her ribs and struggling for breath. She was only a few feet away from the oven and eye level with Perry who was looking directly at her. "Help me," she begged quietly, just barely mouthing the words.

Tears streaked down Perry's clenched jaw as he shook his head in sorrow. He had never felt such sadness and cowardice as he did right then. "I'm sorry," he whispered to her. "I'm so sorry." He wanted to save her so badly, but Perry knew he was no match for Gus, especially without a weapon, and would inevitably meet the same fate. He turned his head away just as two thick, fur-covered legs stepped in front of his friend.

Gus picked Chrissy up by the neck with one hand. He lifted her to his eye level as her legs whipped frantically in the air. As she struggled to break free, the realization sunk in that she was most likely not walking out of that room—and something inside of Chrissy snapped.

All of her fear was replaced with resolve, and she looked straight at Gus with steely eyes. She was not going to give him the satisfaction of seeing her cower for a single second longer. She may have been weaker than him, but she was no longer weak. Chrissy kicked and cussed and punched. She was brave, and she knew where she was going once this life was over. Chrissy spit and Gus squinted as the saliva struck him in the eye.

Even with her ferocious barrage, Chrissy couldn't escape Gus' powerful grip. But she didn't plan on giving up the fight until the fight was over and continued to attack him with whatever she had left. As Chrissy felt the life slowly drain from her body, she channeled all the remaining strength she had into one last shot. She gripped Gus' massive arm and lifted herself up just enough to get one well-placed kick directly to his eyes. It was a fortunate blow and stunned him just enough that he briefly loosened his grasp. Chrissy fell free to the floor and immediately started crawling towards the kitchen door. She could hear his tail slapping against the tiles behind her as she continued on, not yet aware that he had *let* her pass.

Gus simply watched her, like an ignorant kid who tears the limbs off insects and hovers above as they try to crawl away—but all parties in both scenarios knew exactly who was in charge. Chrissy made it to the threshold and pushed open the kitchen door. For a moment, even though deep down she knew it was only false hope, Chrissy felt a modicum of relief laying eyes on the empty game floor. She was halfway out the door when Gus stomped over and grabbed her by the leg. Chrissy screamed and dug her nails into the floor, clawing at it helplessly as he dragged her backwards all the way across the room and dropped her next to the small stovetop oven.

The whole scene unfolded in front of Perry's shameful eyes, but he was even less inclined to do anything at this point than he was before. He forced himself to turn away, weeping silently, unable to bear witness to the consequences of his inaction. But he heard everything.

Gus wrapped his hand around Chrissy's face and slammed her into the stove, shaking the massive vat of marinara that everyone had joyously made dinner with only a short time ago. He placed his hand on top of her skull and gripped so tightly that his claws punctured her skin. Chrissy fought back, just like she promised herself she would, but she was wholly exhausted and knew this was the end. As Gus raised her up, Chrissy willed herself back to the safety of her warm bed, and all was quiet.

Chrissy calmly closed her eyes, and Gus plunged her head deep into the vat of marinara. She flailed wildly, sending blood-red sauce splattering across the white wall. Gus kept her submerged, unfazed as he absorbed the blows and kicks she dealt in retaliation. She tried to break free with every ounce of life left in her, but the might in his one arm outmatched her strength altogether. There would be no fortuitous strike this time—Gus wasn't budging.

Soon Chrissy stopped flailing, and her movements became fewer and weaker. Her body buckled once, then twice, then fell still. Her leg twitched one last time as Gus' tail rose up from the floor and coiled around it like a boa constrictor.

Gus pulled Chrissy's red drenched head out of the vat and dropped her to the floor. He looked down at her beautiful features, partially hidden by long, matted hair; and his eyes were devoid of any emotion. He stood there for so long it was as if he had been put on pause. The dark red sauce was up to his elbow and dripping from his claws, forming a small puddle on the spotless tile floor.

Perry thought about running. His panicked mind raced a hundred miles an hour knowing his next decision could be his last. He ultimately smothered the instinct to flee with the logic that he was still alive and had not been found yet. It was also a much easier route to stay hidden than to jump out and confront a bloodthirsty monster.

Then Perry heard footsteps. Gus was on the move, but Perry couldn't see him from his limited view through the oven window. The footsteps became distant, like he was headed away. *Oh, please, please…* Perry thought.

Suddenly, Gus stepped directly in front of the oven. Perry was so startled that he shot back, making just enough noise that he truly wasn't sure if he'd been heard or not. Gus stood stationary for what seemed like an eternity, save for his tail grazing and bumping against the oven window. There was nothing Perry could do. He just sat there shaking, desperately willing himself invisible. Perry's heart started to thump so hard inside his chest that he could feel the vibrations in his throat. As the noise steadily increased, he was certain the creature could hear it pounding on the other side of the oven door.

Perry's eyes were fixed straight ahead, watching with a madman's anticipation for any kind of movement from Gus. Just when he thought nothing might happen, Gus lifted his arm and wrapped his claws firmly around the oven handle—but he didn't open it. He just bent down until he was eye level with the oven's window, and Perry screamed as he saw his nightmare face to face.

Perry got in fighting position so that as soon as the oven door opened he was ready to go. But the door never opened. Gus looked at him and tilted his head sideways. He placed his hand on the temperature gauge and slowly turned it from zero to the maximum number—600 degrees. He kept turning until the plastic knob snapped off. Perry's eyes widened with fright as he realized what Gus had done.

Perry pounded and kicked hysterically against the door, but Gus effortlessly pinned it closed. "Help!" Perry screamed as Gus observed him with a sadistic glimmer in his eyes. "Help!" he screamed, over and over, as he felt the temperature start to rise.

CHAPTER FOURTEEN

Brad, Ben and Sarah had reached the maintenance room safely and, they hoped, unfollowed. Next to the door was a stand-up cardboard poster of Meaty and The Toppings posed like the cover of The Beatle's *Magical Mystery Tour* album. Brad pointed to the outstretched arms of an overly-smiling Polly. "False advertising!" he exclaimed as he yanked open the door. The three quickly entered the room.

"Lock it," Ben said.

Brad did so and then barricaded himself up against the door. Almost immediately he looked down and spotted a long, rusty crowbar. It was way closer to the length and weight of a baseball bat than the clumsy pole he'd been carrying, and two years on varsity made it an easy decision which one he would be more effective with. He dropped the pole and started doing faux practice swings with the crowbar.

"You guys hurry," Brad said. "We don't want any surprise visitors."

"So you're good then?" Ben asked, acknowledging the newly acquired piece in Brad's hand.

Brad held the crowbar up. "Set. Unless you find a gun in here."

Ben and Sarah started rummaging through boxes and shelves for anything they could use to defend themselves.

"What if we attacked them on stage?" Brad wondered out loud. "I mean, aren't they just standing there?"

"And what if they're not?" Sarah responded. "I doubt they'd just let us walk up and kill them."

"Then light the whole stage on fire," Brad said. "We wouldn't even have to get close."

Sarah dropped a handful of junk and stood up. "Brad. As of now we have no way out of here," she said. "Setting fire to the stage would light the whole building."

Ben found an old, heavy monkey wrench under some rags and interrupted the conversation. "I think this'll work."

"I wouldn't wanna get hit by it," Brad said.

"I can't find anything," Sarah said, pulling useless item after useless item out of a weathered box.

"Grab something. Anything's better than nothing," Ben replied. He reached into another, slightly more hidden weathered box and handed her a hammer.

Sarah performed a few overhead striking motions then approved.

"If we can't find anything else, let's get the others and get out of here," Ben said.

****

As the three of them approached the kitchen, they began to hear muffled screams bellowing out from behind the door. Their cautious steps escalated into a frantic sprint towards the unknown. Brad was the first to peer inside the window and witness the grisly sight.

It took a moment to process Chrissy's lifeless body covered in red liquid on the floor next to a monstrous creature pinning his friend inside a burning oven, but only a moment. "Perry," Brad whispered, his breath fogging up the window. He then sprung into action, bursting through the kitchen door with Ben and Sarah following close behind. Brad charged straight at Gus and uncoiled the steel crowbar across his face. *That big bastard didn't even flinch*, Brad thought as he took a step back from the creature.

"Help me! Please!" Perry cried out, gasping and coughing from the thick, hot, suffocating air inside the oven. Brad looked down and saw Perry up close for the first time, and all sound drowned out. He stood in shock for a mere second too long before the blur of a monster's arm entered his vision and exploded against his chest. Brad flew backwards, landing hard against the tile floor with a thud.

Ben turned to Sarah with a look she had not seen on him before. "Stay back," he said. Ben ran up and smashed the iron wrench down on Gus's arm with all his might, but it did nothing. Gus turned his head and looked directly at Ben.

Oh shit, Ben thought. With one arm, Gus lifted Ben high in the air. He looked down at Gus, eyes filled with awe, totally caught off guard by the strength of the creature. In a violent outburst, Gus crashed Ben down onto the countertop island with such force that his wounded body slid off the other side.

Sarah anxiously watched from a distance. She didn't know what to do. The sound of Perry's tortured screams cut through her frenzied mind, and her eyes locked in on the oven. He was thrashing in absolute agony, his skin starting to bubble. It was a gruesome sight, but Sarah didn't turn away. Even though Ben

127

had told her to stay back, Perry was her friend, and nobody was going to tell her what to do, even with the noblest of intentions. Sarah dashed over to the counter. She tossed the hammer she was carrying and then grabbed the longest blade she could find in a bulky, wooden knife block. She sprinted towards Gus with the knife raised high overhead and plunged it deep into his back. Without so much as a wince, Gus turned around and backhanded Sarah across her side, sending her airborne. She landed fortunately on her shoulder, but the momentum snapped her head hard against the floor. Gus reached behind his back and slid the knife out from where it was lodged, tossing it to the ground. Sarah lay still, feeling as though she had been hit by a truck as she struggled not to black out.

Ben could only listen helplessly to Sarah's attack as he regrouped on the other side of the countertop island. He shook his head until he could see straight again, then grabbed the monkey wrench lying next to him. Ben climbed on top of the island, and as he stepped up to Gus, he felt the potency return to his muscles. He cracked the wrench down on the possum's head so hard that he thought it might cave in.

It only left a dent.

But for the first time in the battle, Gus seemed to be slightly shaken by a blow. Before Ben could attempt another swing though, Gus' massive arm swept across his ankles, sending him falling onto the counter. Gus reared back with a hammer fist and came down towards Ben's head. Ben twisted his body something awkward and practically threw himself off the counter as Gus' fist smashed deep into the metal top, leaving a small crater.

"Brad, get up!" Ben yelled as he positioned himself to the side of Gus. Brad opened his eyes and saw Perry in the oven before him. There was smoke coming out now, and he was burning alive. These monsters had killed two of his friends and were about to kill a third—and Brad saw red. He felt his pulse radiate throughout his entire body as blood rushed to every limb, heating him into a spiral of unbridled rage.

"Hit his head!" Ben yelled out while crashing the wrench down on Gus' arms. Brad snuck up behind Gus and rained down blow after blow on the back of his head. He could feel tense vibrations shoot up his forearm every time the crowbar connected against Gus' metal skull. Inside the oven Perry's clothes ignited, and he was soon totally engulfed in flames. The screams were unbearable.

Sarah was lying on her side, floating in and out of consciousness. Every few seconds, her eyes slowly drifted shut—it was as if she were fighting against invisible lead weights that kept pulling them closed and lulling her into blissful darkness. Everything was spinning in slow motion. The furious battle played out before her on a tilted stage, and all she could do was watch. Passages of calm, blank nothingness, interjected by snapshots of chaos: Ben and Brad, both so brave, unleashing every last bit of their strength and fury against Gus. *Stay awake.* Gus faltering at long last, then staggering one step backwards. *Open your eyes.* Brad seizing the moment of weakness and smashing the crowbar into Gus' face. *Ben needs you.* The monster falling with the force of a centuries-old tree cut down onto the shuddering ground.

Gus lay motionless on the kitchen floor, his eyes closed and his mouth hanging slightly open. Brad threw his crowbar down and immediately ripped open the oven door. The stench of burnt human flesh filled the air. The devastating outcome they'd fought so valiantly to prevent had happened. Brad covered his mouth and turned his head away sharply. The sight of Perry's charred corpse and terror-stricken eyes frozen open in death would be etched in his memory forever. "Perry," Ben sobbed, his voice catching in his throat. The tears blurred out the horrific sight of his best friend, but they couldn't deny Ben from knowing the excruciating pain he must have suffered.

Seeing the anguished looks on Ben and Brad pulled Sarah back from the precipice of unconsciousness. They didn't have to say anything—she knew that Perry had not survived. The grief hit her deep in the chest, almost pushing the life back into her as much as it seemed to take it away. She sat up and met Ben's eye. "Chrissy?" she asked, with equal amounts of hope and dread. Ben looked down and shook his head. Sarah put her hands over her eyes and wept. "No, not her too," she said.

Brad was conditioned from a young age to hide any cracks in his tough exterior. But in this moment, the harder he resisted his emotions, the harder they came, until he finally and fully gave in. Ben squeezed his eyes shut, hearing only the sound of pain. So much pain.

They were all so overcome with mourning their fallen friends that nobody noticed Gus' tail sliding silently across the floor. It lightly wrapped itself around Ben's ankle then clamped down so tightly he felt as if his bone might snap. Ben's head whipped down towards Gus just in time to see the creature's ear twitch. *That son of a bitch was playing poss—*Suddenly Ben's leg was viciously yanked from underneath him, and he collapsed to the floor.

With his tail wrapped around Ben's ankle, Gus jumped to his feet and reached for the ax lying against the wall. He pulled Ben towards him and reared back with the weapon. In a panic, Ben instinctively grabbed the thin air around him for anything to hold onto but could only use his own body's force to slow the momentum. He looked up to see light glint off the sharp blade above and braced himself.

Gus maniacally swung the ax down towards Ben's snared foot. But at the last second he jerked his ankle back as hard as he could, and the blade sliced clean through Gus' gnarly appendage. A throaty screech spewed from Gus' mouth as he watched the disjointed piece of tail writhe around the floor like a decapitated snake.

Ben hastily shuffled backwards as he saw Gus step towards him with the ax. "Ben!" Sarah cried out, and she ran up to help him to his feet. As she bent down, Gus wildly swung the ax at her. Sarah ducked the blade by mere inches, and it ripped into the vat of marinara behind her, exploding the thick sauce outwards in every direction.

Ben struggled to find his footing in the marinara. A hand came out of nowhere and grasped onto the collar of his shirt. "Come on!" Brad yelled as he pulled him out of Gus' reach. The monster shot forward and took an almighty swing at Brad with the ax, narrowly missing again. The blade lodged deep into the metal fridge beside them, and cool air began to seep out of the fracture like smoke. As Gus focused on prying out the ax, Brad and Sarah helped Ben to his feet. Brad looked back and could tell it was only a matter of seconds before Gus reclaimed his weapon. "Let's go!" he shouted.

The boys scooped up their weapons, and they all bolted for the door. In the corner of his eye, Ben saw Sarah turn back. "Sarah!" he called out as he spun around to see her snatching up her knife from the floor. Behind them, Gus pulled the ax out from the fridge, causing the cool smoke to rush out and surround him. His piercing eyes stared straight into Ben's, and for just a moment, they froze in time, adversary against adversary. Gus drew back the ax and aimed directly at Sarah who was running towards the door. "Hurry!" Ben yelled. Gus hurled the ax, and it rotated through the air with astounding speed. The three sprinted through the door just as the ax tore into it. The sheer force of the throw sent the blade straight through the other side as the door flapped in a raving fit.

Ben looked back and saw quick flashes of Gus as the door swept back and forth. Gus had won the battle, but his body wore signs of the heavy price he'd paid. The beating he had taken left huge patches of white fur missing from his head and arms, exposing the mauled metal joints and pistons underneath. He was somehow even more frightening than before.

Gus stood glaring out the door with claws stretched wide. His mouth hung wide open, emitting a guttural hiss. Ben turned his head away from the disturbing sight. "There's another way out of here, follow me," he yelled—and the weary, battered friends raced towards that hope.

CHAPTER FIFTEEN

The group reached the back of the building and paused to catch their breath after the full-on sprint from the kitchen. Ben leaned forward with hands on his knees. He looked over his shoulder to make sure that neither Gus, nor anything else, was around.

Standing before them was Marinara's rear exit. It was a lightly tinted glass door, practically identical to the one in front. Ben grabbed the handle and shook it violently, but as expected, it was sealed tight. He noticed there was a lock, but he had never seen a key to the door before. "Watch out," he said, turning his face away from the glass and striking the door as hard as he could with the iron wrench. It was the same unbelievable result as the front door—the pane didn't even shudder on its hinges.

Fueled by the wave of adrenaline he was still riding from their run-in with Gus, Ben released his frustration on the door. He bashed the wrench into it over and over until his hands were throbbing, but he would not relent. Behind him he could hear Sarah quietly begin to sob, and the weight of it was almost enough to crush him. The tense muscles in his arms suddenly loosened, and the wrench swung down by his side. Then Ben fell to his knees in exhausted defeat.

"Are there any other ways out?" Sarah asked softly, her voice an echo of the faith that was quickly being extinguished in all of them.

"No," Ben replied, hanging his head. How could he possibly save her now? How could he save any of them?

Brad took a long, hard look at the door, searching for answers, and finally came to a conclusion. "It's part of it," he said, slowly backing away from the door with a distraught look. "The whole damn building is part of it. We're gonna die in here."

Hearing both Sarah's tears and Brad's words broke Ben's heart. He was down on his knees, and he too had lost faith. But the tiniest of flames deep inside of him wouldn't be extinguished. There was still so much life at stake. People he held dear were depending on him—and the tiny flame quickly grew into a wildfire. Ben looked up. "We're not going to die," he declared.

"But they'll find us," Sarah said.

Ben stood up, shedding the despair he had felt just a few moments prior and arming himself with the promise to do anything in his power to protect the friends still with him and avenge the ones who were no longer there. "Then we'll slaughter every last one of them," he vowed.

He looked his friends firmly in the eyes, his face reflecting the determination he felt inside. "Right?" Ben exclaimed. "Right?!"

They both nodded, awoken to a newfound sense of hope, and a newfound leader to entrust that hope with.

Ben examined the area around them in search of an idea when something on the floor caught his attention. There was a power drill lying against the wall next to some trim and screws. He picked it up and ran his hand along the cord, thinking hard. Ben looked down at his dress shoes then over to Brad's Nike Air Force high-tops. The idea unfolded in his mind with such eloquence that it seemed predestined. "Brad, what size shoe are you?"

"Ten and a half. Why?" Brad replied.

"I've got an idea," Ben said.

He looked at Sarah. Although she was trying her best to put on a brave front, the knife in her shaking hand betrayed her.

"Mind if we switch?" Ben asked, gesturing to his wrench.

Sarah held out the trembling knife, and Ben took it gently, replacing it with the wrench in her hand. "Better?" he said.

"Yeah," Sarah said meekly, mustering the slightest of smiles.

"Are you okay?" Ben asked.

Sarah gave a nod and Ben wrapped his arms tightly around her. She dug her head into his shoulder. It was the most needed embrace Sarah had ever received.

Afterwards, Ben looked over at Brad.

"Brad?" he said.

"Let's do it," Brad replied, fully restored back to his glorious bravado.

****

Everyone was on guard as they navigated through the gaming floor, looking hesitantly around every machine they approached. Ben stopped abruptly as they passed a trio of arcades. "Wait," he said. He crouched down, focusing on the power socket at the base of the machines. "Even better," he whispered as he tossed aside the drill he'd been carrying. Ben

135

got on his hands and knees and reached behind the arcades with the long kitchen knife.

****

The inside of the men's bathroom was as sterile and clinical looking as a hospital. Ben would know—he was usually the one scrubbing it. Not much thought went into the décor, as evidenced by the plain tile, paint and fixtures. The only thing remotely unique about the space were the two overhead fluorescent lights. For some reason the long tubes were dark blue, probably purchased off a discount rack, and they completely transformed the otherwise bland room into one of heavy mood. A bad connector led to one of the lights flickering continuously, giving the bathroom an eerie strobe effect. There were four stalls, and across from each of them were an equal number of mirrors affixed above porcelain sinks.

The three walked in and each took their post—Ben at the far end of the bathroom near the last sink, with Sarah and Brad both inside separate stalls, standing on top of the toilets.

Sarah leaned forward inside the stall, bracing her arms on the walls so she could peek through the crack where the door was hinged. One of the mirrors was directly across from her, reflecting the blank stall door back at itself. Several minutes passed and Sarah began to wonder if their plan was going to work. Just as she was about to glance at her watch, she detected a sudden movement. Sarah's pulse raced as fright and confusion gripped ahold of her from the soundless image she saw in the mirror—a teenage girl running into the bathroom, bloodied and disheveled. Her pink tank top was torn to shreds, as if she'd been viciously attacked, and she had a huge gash across her torso that was soaked in gore. She was clearly trying to escape from someone or *something* as she looked around in desperation.

Sarah pulled her gaze away from the mirror's reflection to analyze the immediate space right in front of her stall. There was nothing there. She looked back up at the mirror, and there she was again—the blood-soaked girl. Even after all Sarah had witnessed that night, it was still hard to accept what she was looking at. Sarah closed her eyes, trying to reset her vision and prove that it was all in her mind. But when she opened them up, the girl remained. Sarah watched with a heavy heart as the girl clasped her stomach in pain. Although she couldn't hear a thing, it was obvious the girl's breathing was becoming increasingly labored. She was dying.

The girl lifted her blood-covered hands in front of her face, then looked in the mirror. The torment she had endured was fully realized as she saw what they'd done to her. She lifted a finger to the glassy surface and began to form crudely written letters with her own blood.

It was all so sad, and Sarah felt so powerless. Why was this happening? Was it a reflection of the past? Had this all happened before?

The girl finished writing. She braced herself against the sink for support and hung her head. Sarah read the message as streaks of blood dripped down from the letters to the bottom of the mirror. It read:

THEY ARE ALIVE

Suddenly the girl's head whipped around towards the door. Something had made an entrance. Sarah tried every angle to see towards the door, but her sightline was limited only to the mirror in front of her. The girl's body tensed and her mouth opened wide. She was screaming, and sound wasn't needed to feel her fear.

The girl began to cautiously back up, her wide eyes fixed on something terrifying in front of her. Sarah couldn't see what the girl was looking at, but whatever it was did something so menacing that mascara-stained tears began to stream down her face as she shook her head no. Then for some reason the girl stopped, and while her body was still facing the door, her head turned all the way until it was looking right into the mirror beside her. There was a strange calm about her at that moment, and Sarah could swear that the girl was looking straight at her— and then she ran out of view.

Sarah stared forward anxiously, waiting for something else to appear. But nothing did. She was gone. The message was gone too. It was as if nothing had happened.

Just as Sarah was about to ask if anyone else had seen what she just had, the bathroom door slowly scraped open, and she drew herself as far back into the stall as possible. Gus stepped into the bathroom, his burly form filling the entire door frame.

At the far end of the room, Ben stood with one hand behind his back. He appeared relaxed, full of a confidence that had not been displayed until now. In his other hand he restlessly rolled around a balled-up Tootsie Roll wrapper between his fingertips. The sink beside him was turned on high, and gushing water overflowed onto the floor. It was the only noise in the air, and the sound of water crashing against hard tiles closer resembled a waterfall than a sink.

Ben glanced down at the puddle which was steadily

inching larger in diameter. The water had risen to the halfway point of the soles of the Air Force high-tops he was wearing. He looked up at Gus from under his brow. A deranged smile formed on Ben's face. "What took you so long?"

Inside the stalls, Brad and Sarah were alert and ready to attack. Brad clenched his crowbar while Sarah held tight to her knife. Ben's wrench sat behind Sarah on the toilet, for the time safer out of his hands than in them. The plan was good but it was risky. Ben was defenseless, and everyone knew it except the enemy. Brad and Sarah watched the stand-off unfold with strained eyes through the gaps in the stalls.

Gus stomped straight towards Ben who had to suppress the all-consuming instinct to flee. The heavy footsteps got so close that Ben could feel the vibrations underneath him. Then, out of nowhere, Gus stopped. From only a few feet away he looked right at Ben and tilted his head.

Sarah watched nervously as the water puddle crept towards Gus' feet. *Come on, come on,* she thought, willing him to take a few steps forward. But the two remained at a standstill, neither one making a move.

Ben had not anticipated Gus' hesitancy. It was surreal to be right in front of the creature without a fight, much like encountering a docile great white during a dive. He had seen him up close so many mundane times before, but perspective had lent a new view, and now he finally *saw* him.

Ben knew he had to get Gus to come towards him. Without second thought he went with the first thing that popped into his head. "Swing it rat," he said, then flicked the balled-up piece of trash in his hand at the possum's face. Gus reared back the ax and stepped forward. Ben dropped to the floor, taking the severed, sparking cord he'd been hiding behind his back and jamming it into the water at his feet.

There was a sharp crack of electricity, and Gus was frozen in place. Countless volts surged through the thick arcade cord plugged into the wall behind Ben. The current racing through Gus' metal frame caused him to tremor and convulse wildly.

Ben turned to jump out of the puddle—but Gus' hand shot out and grabbed him by the wrist. Ben was suspended in motion as lighting ripped through his body. He couldn't think or move. It was as if his very existence had been put on pause. All he could do was behold the monster that was going to send him to his grave.

Gus painstakingly lifted the ax with his trembling hand, fighting the incapacitating force of the electricity with an unrelenting drive to finish Ben off.

"No!" Brad screamed, bursting out of the stall and bumrushing Gus with the crowbar. He slammed it down on Gus' arm, breaking the connection with Ben but briefly shocking himself in the process. The boys did everything they could to keep their balance knowing a fall would be deadly.

They had barely managed to stagger out of the puddle when Gus came down with the ax and tore it through the wall where Ben had just been standing.

Knowing they were out of harm's way, Ben and Brad fell to the floor as the electricity seeped out of their bodies. Sarah opened her stall and ran to their sides. "Are you two okay?" she asked, kneeling down beside them. They both nodded.

All three of them looked up at Gus as he shredded the ax into the wall over and over, the electricity forcing him into the inadvertent reflex. Gus turned abruptly and smashed his thick arm through the overflowing sink behind him, absolutely obliterating it. Water from the broken pipe shot high into the air.

As he thrashed about uncontrollably, Gus shot the ax up towards the ceiling, breaking one of the two fluorescent bulbs above. The only light remaining in the room was the damaged one, now radiating an intensified dark blue strobe effect over everything. The three watched through entranced flashes as Gus flailed about in agony. The hypnotic lighting was compounded by bursting sparks and water droplets raining down. It was strangely beautiful and horrific all at the same time.

The strength the monster possessed to be still standing was incredible, but it was clear he was not escaping this fate, and time was the only factor. A succession of muffled popping sounds came from within the wall right before the socket shorted out and burst like a firecracker. Gus let out a mechanical shriek and fell to the floor. His smoking body slowly curled up in the water, and he looked directly at the group. Everyone relished the sight of Gus' slow, torturous demise. They couldn't help it after all he had taken from them.

What was left of his contorting tail soon came to a standstill, and he hissed defiantly at them one last time. A permanent emptiness washed over Gus' light pink eyes as his jaw fell open lifelessly.

They all just sat there, nobody saying a word.

Eventually, everyone got to their feet. Brad tapped the toe of his shoe, Ben's shoe, in the water to make sure the current had dispersed.

"Hey, you mind?" Ben said. "Those are real leather."

"Could've fooled me. Now gimme my shoes back," Brad replied.

"I dunno," Ben said, strutting in place. "They do look pretty good on me. You think I could pull them off?"

"Yeah, I do think you could pull them off, and put them back on my feet," Brad said.

Sarah couldn't resist chiming in. "There's a six-foot, smoldering possum in front of us, and you guys are talking shoes."

"Is there ever a bad time to talk shoes?" Brad said.

The boys traded back footwear, enjoying the light moment after the heaviness of what they'd all just gone through together.

Brad walked around Gus to pick up the ax, then stepped over his carcass to rejoin the others. Ben grabbed his wrench, and Sarah held onto her knife. One at a time, they made their way through the bathroom door.

As they filed out onto the gaming floor, Sarah immediately surveyed the surrounding area. Her heartbeat quickened as she looked at the stage. "Oh no," she said as the realization dawned on her.

"What is it?" Brad asked urgently. He turned his head to follow her eyeline. She was looking at the countdown clock and its haunting red numbers.

Her lack of response and worried, distant eyes suggested she was nearing a conclusion about something, and it wasn't going to be good.

49:41. 49:40. 49:39…

"What?" Brad asked, more forcefully this time.

"The clock," Sarah replied. "It's a countdown till each one is released. Forty-nine minutes till showtime."

"So we have forty-nine minutes till the next one comes out?" Brad asked.

"No," Sarah said, looking nervously at all the tall arcades surrounding them. "We have forty-nine minutes till the *last* one comes out."

Law now involved in search for teens

Missing persons case officially declared for the five teenagers last seen Friday the 18th

The 7-11 off Old Mill Road was the last documented location of Jeffrey Lane, age 17; Ricky Summerton, age 18; David Gionni, age 18; Maribelle Hart, age 17; and Jennifer Parks, age 18. They were dropped off there at approximately 8pm by Jeffery Lane's older brother Chris.

At first Chris lied to investigators about having any involvement with the group for fear of getting in trouble over buying two cases of beer for them at the convenience store. As he told detectives everything he knew, a few more details emerged. Chris assumed his brother and friends were heading to "Tree Farm," a nickname for an area teenagers are known to frequent as it's off the beaten path and within walking distance from the 7-11. Being the last person to see the group, police pressed Chris for specifics of what they were wearing and if anything was unusual about their demeanor. "I remember they were all dressed up," Chris said. "Like they were going to a party. They were excited for whatever they were about to do. The only thing I remember anyone wearing was Jenny Parks had on a neon pink tank top because I teased her about it when we picked her up."

Even though over 48 hours have passed since the teens were last seen, law enforcement remains optimistic for their safe return. There are reasons the case has been approached relatively lightly according to Sheriff Roy Dean, and continues to be, even after two days. "Some of our deputies are a little too familiar with some of the boys in that group," Sheriff Dean said. "Not saying they're bad kids, more along the lines of rascals. With that said, it's summertime and sometimes kids will be kids. There's no evidence of foul play, but we're keeping our eyes and ears open. I suspect they're gonna walk up to their parents' houses either today or tomorrow with a spiteful hangover, fully prepared to be grounded for the rest of summer."

Chris Lane shared in the Sheriff's positive outlook towards seeing his brother soon. "I'm sure they'll turn up. I ran away from home for a full week when I was his age. They're just having fun. I'm sure wherever they are, they're having a hell of a time."

If you have any information regarding the whereabouts of any of the people listed in this article, please contact local law enforcement immediately.

CHAPTER SIXTEEN

If Sarah was right, there was already one monster out there and another one soon to come. The group gripped tightly to their weapons as they looked out onto the vast game room before them. It had not yet been tainted by any battles or deaths and looked no different than before the nightmare had begun. Ben could almost see Perry, Chrissy and Keaton walking up to join them, but he knew not to let his mind wander too far off, or he might not get it back.

The lights and sounds of all the games were still as vibrant as ever. What was once such an inviting scene was now more like a death maze. And all the distractions made it that much harder to detect a potentially lurking threat. There were so many spaces. So many hiding spots that could conceal danger.

Time was running out, and the commotion from all the arcades made the idea of a slow, cautious walk through the game room seem pointless, maybe even foolish. Ben racked his brain for a place they could hide and regroup. Somewhere away from the main floor.

"I think we should go back to the maintenance room," Ben said. There were no objections. After all, he was infinitely more familiar with the place than they were. "Are you guys able to run?" They both nodded. "Ok, let's go."

They took off in a mad dash, holding tight to the conviction that if a predator can't catch its prey, it can't kill it. They just hoped one wouldn't step right in front of them. The sprint across the room seemed to go in light speed and slow motion all at once. Flashes of color and sound blurred across their senses as they sped by.

The group finally reached the maintenance room, and Ben whipped open the door. He held it for Sarah and Brad before slamming it shut and locking it behind him. Feeling safe for the moment, they all collapsed against the walls, heaving and panting as the adrenaline receded from their veins.

Brad looked sideways at Ben with a slightly curled lip. "Ben, this is the last party you throw for a while," he said.

"Yeah, I think I'm putting in my two weeks," Ben replied, smiling genuinely for maybe the first time since all of this had started.

Ben slunk down to the floor, and Sarah followed suit, scooting over close to him and laying her tired head on his shoulder. Brad scavenged through the room, not knowing exactly what he was looking for, but looking nonetheless. Having already lightly searched it once before though, he at least knew where *not* to look.

His attention was soon drawn to something in the corner—a large, cylindrical shape hidden under a discarded rag. "Holy shit," he said, stepping towards it. Ben watched curiously as Brad pulled off the dirty rag and revealed the top of a helium tank. "How old is this?" Brad asked.

"We just got it last month," Ben replied, sitting up straight. His interest was now fully engaged, and his mind started ticking.

Brad looked down at him and their eyes met. "Are you thinking what I'm thinking?"

****

It had taken them a little while to get it balanced, but the helium tank was now angled on the floor, resting midway on a step stool that had its stubby legs duct-taped to the floor. The bottom of the tank was tilted up, pointing towards the door. Ben was crouched down on the other end, mock-hitting the nozzle with his wrench over and over in practice swing after practice swing. When the time came, it was one hit he knew he couldn't afford to miss. Surprisingly, Brad was the one providing direction.

"Just come down right there," he said, pointing to the base of a thin metal tube protruding out of the tank. "That should work."

"How do you know all this?" Ben asked, truly impressed.

"Science class. Well, Chad from science class," Brad replied.

"Chad Roark?" Ben scoffed. "Who blows shit up?!"

"The one and only," Brad reminisced. "We have blown up a lot of shit together."

Sarah couldn't help but grin at the comforting normalcy of the boys' conversation.

"So what's the move now?" Brad asked.

"I don't know if we have one," Ben said. "Wait till someone gets here in the morning?"

"What if morning never comes?" Sarah asked. She was met with silence. The boys looked down at the ground. Sarah wasn't sure if they were searching for answers or hanging their heads in discouragement.

Suddenly Brad's head snapped up. "Emily! Emily's supposed to get here at twelve."

"Yeah!" Ben exclaimed. Even if they couldn't get the door open, it was their only hope of communicating with the outside world. Maybe there was a way out of this hell after all. Ben glanced up at an old, dusty wall clock that read 9:05. "That's not right," he said, nodding towards the timepiece. "Anyone got the time?"

Brad glanced down at his watch. "I've got 11:30."

"Wait, that can't be right either," Sarah said. "There's no way we've only been in here for a couple of hours." She looked back up at the wall clock. "9:05, that's the time we got here. I remember seeing it in the truck right before we got out."

"I know what you're thinking," Brad said. "But that clock could've stopped there months ago. Hell, years ago with Ben and The Janitor running this place."

Sarah held out her wrist. The kiddy watch she had gotten from the prize counter read 9:05. "What are the chances this one stopped there too?" she asked.

There was a long pause. A creeping suspicion was entering Ben's thoughts, and he didn't like its implications.

"So why does mine still work?" Brad asked.

"I'm not sure. I'm not sure of anything right now," Sarah said. "But it feels like it's gotta be past 1 a.m. at least, maybe even 2. We've been in this godforsaken place forever."

"I'm telling you, this watch keeps perfect time," Brad said sternly. "It hasn't lost a minute in five years since my Grandpa gave it to me."

They were all thinking the same thing. Someone just had to say it. "I'm pretty sure time in here is messed up," Ben said. "Like it's slowed down or completely stopped."

"I think you're right," Sarah said. "Brad, maybe your watch *is* correct, but only in the outside world. In here, something is very wrong." Unsettling possibilities began to race through everyone's minds.

All the talk of time stretching and stopping made Brad's head hurt. It was all too hard to make sense of, and there was always the possibility that there was no sense to make at all—it just *was*.

Brad lifted his wrist up. "Look, this watch is all we have to go on. So if it really is 11:30 out there, Emily might still be coming."

"He's right," Ben said. "There's no point in trying to figure all this out. All that matters is we're at that front entrance at midnight, or we're gonna lose our only chance."

"There's going to be two of them out there by then," Sarah said, looking towards the door. "How are we gonna get through them?"

Ben looked up and took a deep breath. There had to be a solution. His eyes wandered across the ceiling tiles, and then he spotted it—the air duct. "We're not going to go through them," he replied. "We're going to go over them."

****

"Must go faster," Brad said with a playful huff while hoisting Sarah up to the air duct.

"I'm going to smack you," she replied.

Sarah reached up and pulled away the vent cover, exposing a wide entrance into the duct. Ben held up the kitchen knife,

149

and Sarah carefully tossed it into the opening. She grasped onto the thin, metal edges and pulled herself into the space.

"Think it'll hold us?" Ben asked.

"Yeah, it seems pretty sturdy," Sarah replied.

Suddenly they heard a loud noise from somewhere in the building, and it startled them all.

"We need to hurry," Ben said, glancing nervously at the door.

Brad quickly grabbed ahold of Ben and lifted him up to the opening. Ben got his elbows inside and rested his weight to test the strength of the duct. With a foreboding creak it shifted down slightly. "It's not gonna work," Ben said.

"I'll move further down," Sarah said anxiously, doing so before the words were even out of her mouth. Ben tried again to advance but knew this time with certainty it wouldn't hold him.

"We can't take the chance," Ben said. "You stay up here."

Sarah rushed to the opening. "No!" she said. "I'm not leaving you."

Ben grabbed tight onto her hand. "I can't protect myself unless I know you're safe," he said, the words flowing directly and truthfully from his heart.

Sarah nodded. She trusted him. And although she didn't like it, she knew it made sense. Sarah looked deeply into Ben's kind eyes, and they reassured her. "It's gonna be okay," he said. "I'll be right down here."

Brad looked up at them with a slightly flushed face. "Getting kinda heavy bud."

"Be careful," Sarah said, her eyes hinting at the formation of tears. They let go of their hands but kept their gaze on one another as Brad lowered him down. From the floor Ben glanced up to Sarah with a forced, bittersweet smile. For now she was as safe as she could be, and that gave him comfort.

As Ben turned to Brad, the room plunged into total darkness. "Ben!" Sarah screamed.

Ben could hear her start to rustle above. "Sarah, stay up there!" he shouted.

As they tried frantically to process what had happened, Brad reached out and grabbed onto Ben's shoulder. "Shh," he whispered. "Listen…"

****

The old copper power lever that had brought the building to life earlier that night was ripped out of the wall and lay mangled on the floor. The circuit breaker box was wide open and had deep claw marks ripped through it.

The guts of the breaker were still sparking as thin wires and metal fuses stuck out in disarray. Everywhere was now dark except for the red emergency lights overhead. Scattered throughout the building, they provided just enough glow to see but cast an eerie, unnerving hue over everything below.

Lying on the ground underneath the ravaged electrical boxes was a torn pinstripe suit, shredded to pieces and discarded—like shackles from a prisoner broken free.

CHAPTER SEVENTEEN

Ben and Brad had not dared move at all since everything went dark. They were like a pair of posed statues, listening fixatedly for another noise similar to the mysterious one they'd heard earlier. Sarah was still lingering in the air duct above, patiently waiting for the next move. It was so pitch black inside the small room that it felt like they were lost in the abyss of space, save for the sliver of red light that crept underneath the door.

"Did you hear that?" Brad whispered.

"No," Ben replied. But he wasn't sure if he was listening so intensely in the silence that he wasn't hearing straight at all.

Brad leaned his ear against the door, concentrating to the point that he could feel tension in his head. He couldn't hear a thing.

Then, suddenly—

BOOM!

Something crashed into the door. Something big.

Brad jerked back, his own scream joined in unison by Ben's and Sarah's.

"Get some light!" Ben shouted.

Brad pulled a lighter from his pocket. The small flame

illuminated just enough of the room that the boys could at least see one another and a few feet around them. They sprung into action, knowing exactly what they both needed to do without exchanging a single word.

Ben knelt beside the helium tank and raised the wrench over the nozzle. Brad gripped the ax with his free hand, poised in attack position. Just then, almost too quiet to notice, a faint scratching noise came from outside the door. It sounded like metal against wood and didn't seem to be moving more than an inch up or down. Whatever it was, it was taunting them. And based on the looks in the room, it was working.

Then it stopped.

Ben squinted in the barely lit room; something moving had caught his attention. He waved to Brad and pointed to the bottom of the door where the red light was seeping in. A long, single black claw was tucked under the door gap, sliding slowly and deliberately along the inside. It soon stopped at the middle of the door, frozen maddeningly in place.

After a long pause, it began gently tapping against the inside of the door, as rhythmic and torturous as a ticking clock. The boys looked on, almost as mesmerized as they were terrified. Suddenly, the claw shot back outside the door. A few seconds passed, and then—

BOOM!

It sounded like a battering ram smashing directly into the door. "Get ready!" Brad said.

BOOM!

"Sarah, get out of here!" Ben yelled towards the ceiling.

Every muscle in Brad's body was tense as he unleashed a searing battle scream. His fight or flight response had kicked into high gear, and Brad's response was always to fight.

BOOM!

BOOM!

BOOM!

"Let's go!" Brad shouted.

The door shattered into a hundred pieces, and the boys turned to cover their faces. Framed by the red light stood a black-haired wolf creature with snarling white fangs and outstretched claws. Alfie had found them.

The hellish sight was enough to immobilize even the bravest of men. But Ben didn't have time to be scared. He was working off pure instinct, hoping the practice swings would pay off with his one shot. In this moment of life or death, he was a primal, raging animal himself. Ben let out a furious roar, and in one perfectly precise swing, he slammed the wrench down into the nozzle of the helium tank.

With a metallic clunk the top shot off, followed by what looked like smoke surging out of the opening. The noise was deafening, and the tank started to tremble. All of a sudden it took off like a rocket, flying across the room and smashing square into Alfie's chest. The sheer force of the impact sent him flying backwards and straight through the wall behind him. He collapsed into such a heaping a pile of drywall and wooden beams that it was hard to distinguish him from the debris. The resulting thick cloud of dust mixing with the overhead red light created a nightmarish haze.

As the creature lay stunned in the hallway, Ben and Brad bum-rushed it with weapons raised, hoping to finish it off. Just as they got within striking distance, Alfie flipped onto all fours and savagely lunged at them. Brad grabbed onto Ben's shirt. "Run!"

The boys took off down the hallway at full speed, throwing down lockers and shelves behind them as they ran. Alfie blasted down the hall, chasing his prey on all fours. The obstacles slowed Alfie down but proved nothing more than a nuisance. The hallway let out into the game floor, and the boys ran behind the first bank of machines they could find.

The heavy commotion of the chase gave way to complete silence around them. Pressed up against the machines, neither one said a word. The air they gulped down sounded like it was being projected through a megaphone, at least to them, as they tried to get their breathing under control. After a short while, Ben decided to peek from behind an arcade. Alfie was gone.

"Where is he?" Brad whispered. It was a strange feeling of relief mixed with the anxiety of not knowing.

The boys crept from behind the arcades on high alert, looking over the game floor with weapons held high.

Out of the murky red haze, Alfie's long arm suddenly appeared. His razor-sharp claws tore across Ben's leg, then immediately disappeared into the shadows. Ben fell to his knees, screaming in pain from the fresh wound.

They were sitting ducks and they knew it, barely able to see in the wide-open game floor. Alfie wasn't like Gus. There would be no slow grind. This was an apex predator, and he was hunting like one.

Brad pulled Ben to his feet. "Get my back!" he yelled. The boys stood up against one another, their heads on a swivel for any signs of movement.

But all was still.

Then Ben spotted him, crouched down menacingly on top of an arcade. But something was frighteningly amiss from their previous encounter in the maintenance room. Ben couldn't see the creature's pupils—only a pair of blank, white voids staring back at him. A dark liquid slowly dripped from its long, bared fangs. Before Ben could even scream the words, Alfie leapt off the machine.

"Watch out!" Ben shouted, but Brad never saw it coming. Alfie landed directly on top of him, the massive collision sending all three of them tumbling to the floor. Brad shrieked with pain as Alfie's claws dug deep into his side. He soon realized he was pinned in place under the monster's immense weight.

Alfie lunged at Brad's neck, his fangs glistening like porcelain daggers, but miraculously Brad had held onto his ax. He gripped it for dear life with a hand on each end, keeping Alfie's relentless attack at arm's length. He needed the old, wooden handle to stay strong as it was the only thing between gnashing teeth and his soft flesh.

During their struggle, Brad couldn't help but look deep into the eyes of the bloodthirsty beast mere inches above him. There was something more to them than the glass and paint he saw at first glance, and what he found scared him even more. The dark liquid again fell from Alfie's wild, snapping jaws and spattered all over Brad's face. He knew he couldn't hold on much longer.

Alfie's ferocity and strength were overwhelming as he inched closer and closer to Brad's neck with every lunge. Just as Alfie was about to overtake him, Brad saw Ben looming overhead, brandishing the giant wrench high above his shoulder. Ben swung down with a feral grunt, smashing the weapon directly into Alfie's mouth. The creature bellowed out a horrific sound that was neither animal nor machine as a jagged tooth fell onto Brad's stomach.

In the blink of an eye Alfie turned and slashed Ben across the chest. The sheer force stunned Ben, and he stumbled backwards before falling to the ground. He looked down to see four bloody claw marks ripped across his shirt.

Alfie jumped off Brad and moved towards Ben on all fours, instinctually driven to dispose of the newly wounded, weaker prey. Behind them Brad scrambled to his feet. As Alfie coiled down to pounce, Brad drew back the ax. He buried it so deep into Alfie's side that he couldn't see the steel head any longer, just what looked like a long, wooden limb painfully growing out of his body. Brad pulled out the ax, and the gash of exposed, gnarled metal parts began to fill with the dark liquid. Although the wound was partially hidden by coarse black fur, Brad could tell that he had dealt a severe blow to the creature.

Alfie let out a cavernous howl and leapt over a bank of arcade machines, disappearing out of sight. Ben got up and limped over to Brad.

"You okay?" Brad asked.

Ben ran his fingers over the claw marks across his chest. They looked worse than they actually were. But it had been close. Too close. "Yeah, I think so. You?"

Brad gingerly touched his side and looked down at four puncture holes oozing blood. "I've been better," he said, wincing.

They were interrupted by the sound of creaking metal, echoing from somewhere above them. Across the game floor, Alfie was licking his wounds when he whipped his head up towards the same sound.

It took a second, then Ben realized exactly what it was.
Sarah.

****

Inside the air duct, Sarah had been crawling towards a light she saw in the far distance. She hoped against all odds that it led to the exterior of the building. And although she painstakingly tried to avoid making any sounds, she decided it was worth the chance and moved forward.

No matter how far forward she moved though, the light never seemed to get any closer. It was almost as if the tunnel kept stretching itself out imperceptibly so that the light ahead always stayed just out of reach. Sarah was both mentally and physically exhausted and knew it was well within reason she was just seeing things in the dark passageways. She was also keenly aware of what building she was in and what it had already shown itself capable of. But Sarah moved onwards towards the light, determined to find out what it was one way or another.

****

"What was that?" Brad asked, perplexed by the creak they all heard from above.

"I think Sarah's somewhere in the room," Ben said gravely.

The boys looked at one another, both coming to the realization at the same time. If *they* had an idea where Sarah was now, chances were, so did *he.*

Ben's heart thumped heavily in his chest as he looked above. "Sarah!" he called out. "Do not move!"

"It's in the room!" Brad added. "Don't say anything!"

Ben could only hope she'd heard them, so as not to further betray her location. Even if she hadn't, he knew she was too smart to risk making another noise right now. And she didn't let him down.

All was quiet in the building. The kind of intense quiet that makes one yearn for a sound, any sound at all, to calm the penetrating anticipation of the next thing to come.

Ben didn't know exactly what he was waiting for to happen. At that specific moment, he had absolutely no idea what to do. His mind was barraged with hurried questions, one sparking right into the next. *Should we try to find her? Or would that put her in more danger? Should we get her out of the ducts? Create a distraction? She's still safest up there, right?*

Before he could properly formulate a decision, there was a sound.

Thunk.

The screen of a nearby arcade came on.

Thunk.

Thunk.

Thunk.

Row by row, the screens lit up on every arcade in the building. No beeps and pops. No flashing lights. Just blank, glowing screens on every one. The strange noise they made grew louder as some sort of energy coursed through them. But it wasn't electricity. The power in the building remained off, with everything still pitched in red obscurity. A single message warned ominously in white letters on every single screen in the room:

GAME OVER

Ben swallowed hard. A cataclysm was looming, he could feel it. And soon he could hear it. A faint tapping drifted from the stage area. It was the sound of a drumstick softly rapping against its instrument. All the other monsters had silently slunk off the stage and into the shadows, unknown to anyone, biding their time to attack. But this one, this *last* one, wanted them to *know* he was coming. He was proudly announcing his impending arrival, and there wasn't a damn thing they could do about it.

The tapping grew louder, and the tempo increased. Despair poured over Ben and Brad as they both knew exactly what this meant. The king was stepping off his throne. Meaty was coming.

CHAPTER EIGHTEEN

The countdown clock above the stage flashed one minute remaining. A muffled tap accompanied each passing second. The thick velvet curtains drew open, ceremoniously revealing the hulking silhouette of the main attraction. A single spotlight clanked on from above and bathed Meaty in a perfect circle of illumination. His head was down, zeroed in on the drum set before him which he rapped slowly and methodically. With each tick of the clock he tapped a little harder and a little faster than the one before. The noise and pace kept building, building, building…

As the clock reached the final ten seconds, Meaty tossed the sticks to the ground and began pounding the drums with his bare fists. They tore through the skins of the instrument before crushing straight into the metal frame itself. Insatiable hate coursed through each and every powerful strike, and the drum set began to wilt and tear. Pieces flew everywhere as the brute relentlessly pummeled down. Soon it was completely demolished, and Meaty sat with his arms hanging down, calmly looking over the disarray he had created. His crown shimmered, still placed perfectly atop his head.

"It's showtime!" blared from the speaker, and Meaty looked up towards the spotlight. He closed his eyes and basked in the warmth, satisfied that his time had finally come. He stood up and trampled straight through the pieces of drum set as he made his way to the edge of the stage.

Meaty jumped off, landing with a monstrous thud into an area of the dining pit where light couldn't quite reach. A shade darker than coal, he blended right in with his new surroundings. Ben and Brad could feel the aftershock as they looked on in awestruck terror from above. Meaty glanced towards the gaming floor and began stalking towards his audience.

****

While they should have been running for their lives, the boys remained curiously still. Even though they had already encountered three of the monsters, they had never seen one come to life right in front of them. It was like watching a stone gargoyle shake off the last century and begin to spread its heavy wings. To behold it, regardless of its intentions, was simply extraordinary.

In the distance a towering figure materialized out of the darkness. As it approached, the shadow began to take shape and reveal itself—bristly, black fur cloaking a muscular, almost humanlike form, but bigger, *much bigger*. As the behemoth neared, Ben should have feared for his safety. But the only thing he could think about was Sarah. She needed him. He had to stay alive for her.

"Oh man," Brad said, not able to take his eyes off Meaty who was drawing closer with every step.

Meaty's steady stride broke into a sprint, and he charged directly towards them. "We got company!" Brad shouted, and the boys turned to run.

With deceptive speed, Meaty was right behind them in an instant, hovering like a dark storm cloud. His stature was immense, dwarfing the other animatronics by a good measure. He was at least seven feet, if not a shade taller.

Ben looked behind him to see just how close Meaty was. He only needed to turn a few inches before the visage of the beast exploded into his peripheral vision. Meaty was right beside him and immediately backhanded Ben across the chest, sending him flying through the air and crashing into the glass prize counter. Ben gasped for breath, rolling around in a thousand pieces of glass.

Brad recklessly swung his ax, but it came to a dead stop as Meaty intercepted it mid-air. Although he tried with all his might to tug it back, Meaty easily pulled it out of his grasp and hurled it across the room. Brad knew his only option at that point was to run, but Meaty was too close and grabbed him by the shirt. As Brad struggled to break free, Meaty formed what seemed to be a smile, relishing the utter dominance over his victim.

Without a hint of strain, Meaty raised Brad off the floor with one hand. In a sudden, seamless motion he swung him overhead at full velocity and slammed him face-first into the ground. It was a move that easily could have resulted in a broken neck, but Brad landed fortunately and was left only stunned.

At the prize counter Ben pushed himself up to a sitting position as tiny shards of glass sliced into his palms. His head was spinning, but he was too fueled by adrenaline to feel either the pain of the fall or the several long cuts on his skin. He looked around for his wrench, but it was nowhere in sight. Then his eyes locked in on the ax lying not far away.

Brad, still reeling from the assault, was lying completely helpless on his side as Meaty stood looming over him. From the edge of his horizontal viewpoint he saw an enormous foot thundering down straight towards his face. His body reacted quicker than his mind as he rolled out of the way and felt a whoosh of air from behind his head. He heard the loud crack of wood fracturing as Meaty's foot tore straight through the floor.

With Meaty temporarily stationary, Ben saw his opening. He snuck up from behind, holding the ax. Thinking back to Polly's demise, he figured if he could get a good swing at Meaty's neck, then he could end it all right there.

Ben drew back and swung. As the blade cut through the air, he saw Meaty's head slightly flinch. At the last possible moment Meaty's forearm shot up, and the ax tore into it. Unfazed, the monster turned his head towards the chunk of steel lodged within his arm, and Ben was left staggered. Meaty moved his arm from the side to his front as Ben held tight onto the handle, not wanting to relinquish possession of the weapon. But Meaty had another idea.

With the blade still wedged firm, Meaty brought over his free hand and smashed down on the handle, splintering it clear in half. As the ax head fell to the floor, Ben looked down at the useless piece of wood in his hands. Before he could look back up, Meaty was out of the hole and facing him. Ben backed up gently, as if he had stumbled upon an ill-tempered grizzly in the woods.

Brad had managed to get to a knee when he happened to glance into the hole that Meaty had left. He leaned in close, inexplicably drawn to its beckoning. It was ink black inside, but it kept intensifying, getting darker and darker until it became a color he had never seen. It was beyond imagination, and as much as he tried, Brad couldn't pull away. Then an image slowly started to appear. Deep in the black abyss he saw his future.

As Ben walked backwards Meaty advanced, step for step, never letting him get farther than striking distance. Ben knew Meaty was just toying with him and that as soon as he initiated the only option he had, Meaty would end it. But Ben was growing tired of Meaty's taunt and decided if this was the end, then it would be on his own terms.

He pivoted as fast as he could, but before he could even get fully turned around, Meaty caught him with a vicious uppercut. The colossal fist landed square under Ben's chin, sending him airborne like a rodeo cowboy getting the full brunt of a pissed off bull. He smashed back-first into the screen of a Galaga arcade, sending thick pieces of glass and sparks exploding in a flash of blinding white light. Meaty threw his forearm in front of his eyes, caught off guard by the sudden glare.

Ben was out cold as gravity took over, and his body slid down the front of the arcade. He slumped down like a ragdoll, settling in an awkward sitting position against the machine. Meaty hovered over Ben's limp body, as if contemplating the final blow that would surely kill him.

Brad got to his feet and saw Meaty standing over his friend. *It's no different than practice*, Brad told himself. *Just go!* He dug his foot into the floor and took off in a blur. Leading with one of his broad shoulders, Brad coiled up right before impact. He blasted into Meaty with a form football tackle, ramming him so hard against a wall that a cratered imprint was left behind.

Brad took a couple steps back from his nemesis. With the back of his hand he wiped the spit from the side of his mouth. "Told you I'd jack you up," he said as arrogantly as he possibly could.

Meaty's reaction was so unexpected that it took Brad by surprise. The monster just stood against the wall staring at him. His eyes were so wide as they bore into Brad that they looked as if they might pop out of his head. Brad knew he had not physically injured Meaty, but he may have hurt his pride just a little.

Having no previous experience in such an unusual standoff, Brad's natural inclination was to stare right back.

And so there they stood.

Meaty broke first, turning his head to the side and shifting his gaze to where Ben lay unconscious.

"Hey!" Brad shouted, commanding Meaty's attention right back towards himself. "Aint nothin' to see over there. I'm the one you want." He popped the sides of the collar on his letter jacket. "All-state motherfucker!"

Meaty stepped away from the wall and stalked directly towards Brad, who smartly kept a fair distance from his adversary this time. "That's it," Brad goaded. "That's it."

Meaty picked up his stride, and Brad subtly nodded. "Okay," he whispered. Then, turning on a heel, he jetted away from his pursuer. Brad ran up to the big, yellow square at the edge of the game floor and practically threw himself down the slide. As soon as his feet hit the dining pit he crouched down and ran alongside the cafeteria tables until he disappeared into the red darkness.

Meaty took the stairs, skipping over two at a time as he walked down. He surveyed the dining pit, then leisurely headed over to the first row of tables and placed his outspread hand under one of the orange colored edges. In one upward motion, he launched the entire ten-foot table in the air like a plastic toy. It crashed down in a heap of twisted metal on the other side of the pit. He followed suit with the rest of the tables, one by one, row by row. Brad peeked out from where he was hiding at the side of the stage. The devastating show of force and earsplitting noise felt like a tornado had come down right on top of him.

Brad knew he had already taken enough risk by peeking out once. He drew back tightly against the safety of the stage, now focusing on the front door which he had a straight-line view of. He looked down at his watch—it read 11:55. *She's almost here,* he thought. *Just a few more minutes.*

Brad remembered time was almost assuredly moving slower within Marinara but held firm to the belief that his watch was keeping up perfect with the outside world. Nevertheless, the ticking seconds felt like they were going in slow motion. *C'mon,* he silently urged, willing midnight to come quicker. *C'mon!*

****

Sarah had been frozen in place since the boys shouted up their urgent warning. She had heard some of the earlier commotion below but couldn't figure out where exactly it was coming from or who exactly was making it. Only a couple feet in front of her was a vent, imploring her to look through it and hopefully find the answers to her questions. She inched forward as lightly as she could until she came upon it. Sarah looked down between the metal slats but didn't see much of anything. She soon realized she was over a wide-open area of the gaming floor.

Just then, a shadowy figure passed into view. It was too dark to make out any detail, but there were only two options left and the lean frame gave it away—Alfie.

He paced in and out of Sarah's line of sight. Each time she hoped that he would keep going, but each time he returned. Sarah held her breath as he walked right below her and stopped. She gripped tightly onto the knife, praying he wouldn't sense her presence. She wasn't sure if he had tracked her scent or heard her, or if it was just pure coincidence he had stopped where he had. It didn't really matter. He was there. Every nerve inside of her was on edge as she focused on not making a sound.

Sarah watched as Alfie's body abruptly went rigid, like an abductee frozen in an alien tractor beam. He began to slowly tilt his head back, and Sarah quickly moved out of sight. It kept going back until he was looking directly up at the vent. His eyes rolled back in his head as if he were possessed—two blank, white ovals lay transfixed on his face.

As his pupils slid back into place, one eyelid began lazily closing just as the other fully opened. They took turns alternating in this unsettling pattern, much like an old, broken doll flipped upside down.

Suddenly, Alfie's eyes snapped wide open. Without warning he leapt straight up in the air and wrapped an arm around the shaft of the vent. The whole section instantly came crashing down with Sarah and Alfie landing in a heap of metal mere feet from each other.

For a brief spell neither one of them moved. Sarah opened her eyes to a swirling haze of red-tinged dust. She turned to find her field of vision suffocated by black fur and fangs.

Fear and instinct expelled whatever lingering buzz she had from the fall, and she shot right up. Sarah clambered to her feet and took off as fast as she could. She didn't look back as she heard the monster begin to stir about in the rubble.

Alfie curled his long fingers around the metal knife that had conveniently fallen right next to him. He stood up and immediately scanned for Sarah in the barely lit room. He swiftly turned to his right and then his left as the swarming red dust mocked his every movement. The side of Alfie's lip quivered as it rose above a crooked fang. He uttered a low, deep snarl knowing she had escaped him. For now.

CHAPTER NINETEEN

Sarah ran with wild abandon, her eyes searching desperately for a safe haven to turn to. She screamed out for Ben, not knowing he was still lying unconscious. She screamed out for Brad, but he couldn't hear her cries with Meaty still in the throes of his dining pit rampage. Sarah had never felt so alone. She would soon have company though, as unwelcome as it might be.

Alfie was hunting her on all fours. She could tell by the rhythm his feet made as they struck the ground. And if she could hear that, then he was close. Sarah didn't need to turn her head to see just *how* close. It wouldn't change anything anyway—she couldn't run any faster. All Sarah knew was that she had precious seconds left before piercing claws dug deep into her back and dragged her down. Then an idea came to her.

She ran towards the tube maze. Alfie was right behind her, audibly huffing in hot pursuit. The round, plastic opening materialized out of the crimson fog, and Sarah leapt into it like a lion through a circus hoop. She landed hard inside but didn't have time for pain. She was still way too close to the opening, and if Alfie grabbed ahold...

Sarah hurled herself forward with reckless disregard, and

not a moment too soon. Right then Alfie appeared at the edge of the opening, his face and outstretched limbs engulfing the entire entrance. His fangs glistened as he smoldered and seethed with rage. A menacing growl followed by a bone-chilling scream intertwined and echoed throughout the space of the hollow tube. Alfie locked eyes with Sarah, his glare soaked in bloodlust. He shot forward, fully primed and yearning for the slaughter. Sarah turned her head and braced for the end.

But nothing happened, save for an intense thumping that rattled her down to her core. She opened her eyes to see Alfie launching himself at the entrance, but he couldn't get through—his shoulders were too broad. He tried to contort his body, but if he had one disadvantage, it was that metal was unforgiving when it came to bending.

Like a rabid animal, Alfie rammed into the opening over and over, his gnashing jaws splattering dark liquid all over the tube. The whole maze shook from the impact, sending years of neglected dust cascading down like a toxic, grey snowfall. Then suddenly he relented, keeping his eyes fixed on Sarah as he moved back in temporary defeat.

Sarah turned forward and began crawling as fast as she could on her hands and knees. The air inside the tube was hot and thick. Subconsciously she recalled the familiar, distinct scent of these very same plastic tubes from a childhood playtime a lifetime ago. Not even in her scariest dreams as a little girl could she have conjured up the nightmarish predicament she was embroiled in now.

Sarah reached what she thought was the middle of the maze and stopped to catch her breath. The yellow walls of the tubes were just opaque enough to light her way but not enough for her to see out of. For the time being she felt a sense of security encapsulated inside of them. It was only slightly more rational than the feeling of protection a child might get by pulling the blanket over their head to hide from a monster. Only this time Sarah's monster was very real, and it was coming to kill her.

Sarah stayed alert for any signs of movement outside the tube, but the darkness wasn't making it easy. She hoped that same darkness would help aid in concealing her too.

Just then the tube shuddered as if something had fallen on it somewhere down the line. Sarah realized almost immediately that nothing had *fallen* on it—something had *jumped* on it. There was a loud thud, and the tube shook again. Then another, but this time it seemed farther away and higher. Alfie was leaping from tube to tube, making his way to the top of the maze.

As if trickling through a canopy of trees, the already faint light from above had only further dispersed the deeper Sarah went into the maze. From his new, brighter vantage point Alfie could see everything below him at once. He just had to wait for movement, something to catch his eye.

Sarah had no idea where Alfie was. She patiently stayed still, hoping he would show his play—but he was more patient. Alfie was a hunter, and within that building's walls he had all the time in the world.

Several minutes passed without any sign of threat, and Sarah could only wait so long. She couldn't stay in there forever, and she knew Ben and Brad were still out there, hopefully alive.

Under the cover of darkness, she started crawling again, ever so slowly and with as little sound as possible. She moved undetected until she came up to a crossroads in the maze that gave her pause. It wasn't the decision of going left, right or forward that made her apprehensive though. It was the transparent bubble protruding from the top of the intersection. She knew that in an instant all of her cover could be blown. But she had moved so far in the maze that going backwards was more of a risk than going forward.

Sarah turned onto her back and slid into view just enough for her to see above. Her eyes followed the yellow tunnels every which way, until she spotted him, perched on a section high above. Before she could get out of sight, Alfie looked down directly at her. They both froze in place as fear washed over Sarah's whole body. Alfie had her in his crosshairs, and she didn't dare look away.

Sarah could only watch as Alfie leapt down, heading for her like a missile. He landed with a massive thud perfectly on top of her tube. The sudden impact jolted Sarah, and she screamed as she once again was face to face with the unrelenting, maniacal black wolf. Sarah frantically clambered forward as fast as she could, trying her best to get out of sight.

But it was to no avail. Alfie could see just enough of her shadow moving right below him. The steel blade of the knife she once held punctured a hole right in front of her, narrowly missing her temple by inches. Sarah crawled at a mad pace as the knife slashed down repeatedly, nearly grazing a different part of her each time. She tumbled down several declines inside the tubing and changed direction at every intersection she could. Alfie tried diligently to stay on her trail, jumping over and diving under the twisting obstacles in his way.

Sarah wasn't sure if it was her erratic scrambling or the absence of light deep in the maze, but after a minute passed without the knife stabbing through the tube, she realized she had finally lost him.

Alfie thrashed and grunted on a nearby section of the maze, whipping his head around for any sign of a shadow moving inside the tunnels. In her frenzied escape, Sarah had unwittingly discovered the lower of the two openings that let out into the ball pit. She crept to the edge of the tube and looked around for the nearest exit. Netting surrounded the entire pit save for one small cutout in the middle of the mesh wall adjacent to her. The only problem was the exit was so far away that Alfie would assuredly see her wading towards it. If she stayed in the maze though, she knew he would find her sooner or later. Inside the ball pit Sarah could hide and have a decent chance to outlast him. At least that's what she told herself seeing as it was the only option before her.

Sarah crawled to the very end of the tube and began untying her sneaker. She reared back and threw it as far as she could down the tunnel. It landed a good distance away, and almost immediately Sarah heard the heavy thuds of Alfie leaping from tube to tube towards it.

Sarah quietly eased herself down into the ball pit. She stayed low and worked her way towards the middle where it was the deepest and she could be fully submerged. As she covered herself and sunk lower and lower, Sarah could hear Alfie slashing and ripping apart the tube, snarling in fury when he didn't feel his blade tear into human flesh.

****

Meaty stood in the middle of the dining pit, his massive shoulders hunched and heaving as he inhaled and exhaled.

174

Surrounded by overturned tables he looked like the lone survivor of a battlefield massacre, standing tall amidst the destruction. Somehow, even in his momentary failure, Meaty still appeared victorious.

Brad remained crouched down at the side of the stage, itching to venture another peek around the edge but resisting the temptation. He glanced down at his watch—it read 12:08. Brad hung his head. *Emily. Where are you?* he thought, as images of her filled his mind.

Brad could no longer hear Meaty rustling about. In a room with three humans being hunted by two monsters, it was unbelievably silent. He leaned against the stage, fully braced for the beast to appear around the corner at any second and snatch him up.

Brad had almost convinced himself of that outcome when a muffled voice came from the front door.

"Hey guys," Emily called out. "Are you in there?"

Brad's head whipped up at the sound. His heart felt like it had leapfrogged inside his chest and slammed up against his ribcage. *Emily!*

Brad could see her clear as day. She was peering through the glass door, her brow furrowed and her nose scrunched as she squinted to see. She was holding her hands on either side of her face as she pressed up against the pane, shielding it from the flood light affixed to the exterior of the building.

Brad looked down at his watch: 12:10 a.m. *Ten minutes late.*

"Right on time," Brad whispered, smirking at Emily's endearing trait of being on 'woman-time' as usual.

Even though Brad knew what stood between him and the front door, as well as what fate quite possibly awaited him when he got there, he'd made up his mind a long time ago what he would do if it got to this point. He snuck one quick glance around the stage and, to his relief, saw that Meaty had his back to him on the far side of the pit. Brad took a deep breath and stood up.

He began gingerly crossing the dining pit like it was covered with rice paper, never once taking his eyes off Meaty. But either by chance, sheer bad luck or the fact that Brad was never able to do anything quietly in his life, Meaty turned around. Brad gave him a half-assed wave and then bolted across the dining pit floor as fast as he could. Meaty took two booming steps forward, then began trudging through the wreckage of the dining pit.

Brad's path took him directly by the smashed prize counter. In a minor stroke of fortune, a small, wooden baseball bat branded *Marinara Slugger* lay amongst the debris. He reached down and grabbed it without missing a beat and barreled towards the front door.

He reached the building's entrance and grabbed onto the door's metal handle, shaking it like he was trying to rip it off its hinges. "Emily!" he shouted. "We're here! We're inside!" He could see her face clearly, just inches from his own, and yet she still squinted as if she couldn't see her boyfriend standing right there in front of her.

Emily leaned back from the still, plain door and huffed as she put her hands on her sides. She tapped her toe against the ground for every annoying second that passed, trying to remain patient as she waited to hear the lock click from the inside. Then she would roll her eyes at Brad and give him a little sass before smiling and asking for a beer. But there was no click or any other sounds at all for that matter. She made a fist and pounded against the door. "Where the hell are you guys?" she called out.

The crushing reality was finally setting in on Brad. This was it. This was *the* plan. And there were no others. Here he was, the only one to get to the door at the exact time he was supposed to be there. He had made it. And now he got to be the only one to see firsthand the truth—that no one could see them and no one could hear them. He wasn't sure what fate had befallen his friends. He was just thankful they weren't there to share this moment of despair.

Brad heard something behind him and looked over his shoulder, but he didn't see anything in the hazy, red darkness. He had been so singularly focused on his task that he'd temporarily forgotten the predator he left behind in the dining pit. Turning back to the door with gritted teeth, he cursed the godforsaken building that had imprisoned him.

Brad struck the baseball bat into the door pane over and over, each impact sending the bat bouncing off the glass as if it were made of rubber. He knew there was almost no chance at all of breaking the door, but almost was all he had left. Brad's swings eventually began to slow down. Sinking his shoulders in resignation, he put a hand on the glass pane. "Emily. I'm right here," he said.

In the reflection of the door, Brad saw the muddy outline of a massive gorilla materialize behind him. He immediately turned and uncoiled the bat as hard as he could across Meaty's iron jaw. With a deafening crack it shattered, sending tiny wooden fragments exploding everywhere. Meaty didn't even so much as blink as the shards lodged into his face and thick, black fur. He just took a long look down at Brad, taking in the sight of the one who had eluded him until now.

Brad was tall and muscular, but standing chest to chest in front of Meaty made him feel small. His pride, however, would not bow down—that was as tall as the ceiling. With his hands shaking by his sides, Brad held Meaty's unwavering stare, not once breaking eye contact.

"Brad?" Emily called out from behind him. He turned towards the door, knowing full well what would likely happen next. He just wanted to look at her one more time. Brad had a fleeting hope that she had seen him at last, but once he saw her expression of disappointment and searching, he knew.

Then something occurred to him that hurt worse than every cut and bruise he had endured up until then. She must have thought he'd forgotten about her.

Brad could be a lot of things. Emily was usually the first to let him know about them. Not because she was mean, but because she was the only girl to give a damn enough to care. She knew deep down who he really was, the man very few others got to see.

Brad could be a lot of things, but he could never forget her.

He looked longingly into her eyes, and for the briefest of moments he could have sworn that she looked right back into his. It was enough. He knew she couldn't hear him, but he whispered the words to her anyway. Out of the corner of his eye, he saw a fist the size of a brick come flying in.

The weight of the punch fractured Brad's cheekbone and came just short of knocking him out cold. But Meaty had held back. He wanted to enjoy this. Meaty grabbed onto Brad and spun him around. He dug his thick, blackened nails deep into Brad's biceps and slammed him against the door. The monster

178

reared back and sunk a right hook directly into Brad's chest. The impact was so intense it felt like his organs were dislodged.

Brad gasped for air as a tiny trickle of blood dripped from his mouth past his chin. His body gave out and tried to fall but a mammoth, outspread hand placed firmly on his chest prevented it. Meaty leaned him back against the door until he could stand on his own. He lifted Brad's arms by the wrists and shook them, much like a ref would do to a fighter to see if they had anything left. He carefully folded Brad's fingers until they made fists and let him go.

Brad could barely stand, but still he stood, swaying defiantly in front of his executioner. He flailed out a punch with such little force that it didn't even hurt when his fist connected with Meaty's granite-hard chest. Brad landed a few more airy, pathetic swings until Meaty grew tired of his own game. He was done holding back. Meaty punched Brad in the face, this time completely obliterating it, then pummeled him with a barrage of crushing strikes against his ribs, chest and stomach. The punches were so relentless and powerful that they held Brad's limp body upright against the door. The magnitude of the beating was astounding.

Finally, Meaty ceased. Broken and battered, Brad collapsed to the floor.

Outside, the crickets chirped their familiar song as Emily folded her arms across her chest. "I'll see you at midnight," she scoffed, mocking Brad's exact words from earlier that day. Her annoyance began to give way as she glanced down and sighed. "Could have at least waited till I got here before passing out," she said. Emily began walking towards the parking lot. After a few steps, she stopped and looked back at the door, her voice soft as she spoke. "I hope you're having a great night in there…"

Brad watched her walk away and fade into the night. He rested his head on the floor and cracked a weak smile. As he grew weary, he felt comforted to have shared one last interaction with her, even if it was one-sided.

Meaty's foot stomped down on Brad's spine, and he realized instantly that he could no longer move. He could only lay there and absorb the blows, incapacitated like a helpless animal. Even knowing what he knew, Brad had still tried to reach her, and that was something he could die with.

Meaty rained down on him like a primal silverback gorilla, raising his fists high above his head then crashing them down onto Brad's back over and over again. He could no longer feel the pain, just dull pressure letting him know what was happening. Suddenly, his neck violently snapped back and the suffering was over. Brad's eyes slid closed as the last flutter of life drifted through his splayed-out hand. He still had the slight smile though. It was worth it.

Meaty's eyes rose up from Brad's body until they were looking straight ahead out the glass door. A look of tempered curiosity formed on his face as he observed the world on the other side. At the edge of the vast, black floor he saw curtains swaying in unison. High above, a legion of white holes punctured the darkness. The main origin of light revealed itself, overseeing everything, yet hiding behind the creeping shapes. In the distance he heard an endless chorus, echoing from seemingly everywhere. For a while he stayed there, not moving anything except for his eyes.

Meaty looked down at the floor. Blood was seeping into a puddle, and it had worked its way to the tip of his foot. He took a step back, and it was then that he saw his reflection in the glass door, possibly for the first time. He slowly raised his hands above his head and watched his other self do the same.

As Meaty lowered his hands, they grazed the sides of his crown and he gripped it tight. He moved it back to its proper resting position, perfectly cocked to the side of his head. Out of nowhere he threw a lightning quick punch into the door, leaving a hairline crack. There was still work left to be done.

CHAPTER TWENTY

For the first time since his forearm was struck with the ax, Meaty stopped to inspect the damage it had left. He lifted his arm and watched as dark liquid oozed from his exposed metal innards down to his hand. Globs of it had already begun to congeal on the surface of his now matted fur. He turned his arm over several times, opening and closing his hand while doing so. It wasn't a critical wound, but it was a wound nonetheless, and Meaty wanted to be at full strength for the final act.

He set course towards the dining pit. As he lumbered across the gaming floor, Meaty came up to Ben's unconscious body splayed out where he'd left him. He walked right past the boy as if he were of no consequence at all. There would be no sport in killing a defenseless creature.

After reaching the dining pit, Meaty climbed onto the stage and headed for the trap door. He threw open the flap and stepped down onto the staircase, his broad shoulders barely clearing the width of the opening.

The red glow from the emergency lights above trickled down the staircase like a silent stream, and it was just enough to illuminate the room as he looked around. Meaty walked over to the impaled heads of past versions of his bandmates and stood over them for an elongated period of time.

He looked up at the wall that was adorned with the disembodied, animatronic limbs. There was an assortment to choose from, all crudely nailed in a row like nightmarish Christmas stockings. Among them was a long, lean arm, clearly belonging to a version of Alfie, that had what looked like thick canvas needles protruding out from where the claws should be. Another was the bare, metal skeleton of an unfinished Meaty arm—he could tell from the black fingernails and patches of familiar fur haphazardly glued about.

Meaty ransacked the room as he considered his choices. He chaotically rummaged through all the electrical clutter and broken-down appendages on the shelves before tossing the shelves themselves to the ground. He was searching for something else, something more. In a locked trunk in the corner of the room, he found it. Meaty wiped off the accumulation of dust-covered junk from atop the battered, leather container and ripped off the lock with his bare hand. He opened the top and looked inside. It was exactly what he was looking for.

Meaty wrapped his fingers around the shoulder of his injured arm and pulled. A dull, metallic crunch from underneath his fur suggested he had dislocated the main socket. A secondary pull tore the flesh and ripped the remaining metal parts that had affixed the limb. He dropped it to the floor, kicking it aside dismissively as it twitched in protest.

With a gaping hole in his side, Meaty took the new limb out of the trunk and popped it into place. He was whole again.

****

A cloak of threatening silence hung over the ball pit where Sarah remained fully submerged. While the dim red light lent a murky cover, it didn't offset the fact that she was still hiding in plain sight. And Sarah was well aware that she had nothing to protect herself with if Alfie were to find her. She fought back the crippling anxiety that sought to wrack her body into a fit by concentrating solely on being absolutely still. Even the shallowest of breaths could shift one of the balls surrounding her and send off a sound-flare announcing her location.

Sarah was angled just enough for her to see out of the pit through a slight gap between several of the balls. In her limited field of view were many of the arcades, although she was so low that she could only see slightly more than the top half of them. She saw Paperboy and Super Sprint. She saw Galaga—and when her eyes traveled down, she almost blew her cover. It was Ben, leaning unconscious against the machine. If the blood and bruises were removed, it would have almost looked as if the night had proceeded as planned.

Sarah couldn't see below his shoulders and worried he wasn't breathing. She focused so strenuously on seeing if he was that her eyes began to ache.

He was a ways away but just close enough that Sarah took the slim chance that he could hear her. "Ben," she whispered, so quietly that she wasn't even sure if any sound had come out of her mouth at all. Maybe she had only felt her lips form around the thought of his name. Tears welled in her eyes. He was right there.

Her instincts were dueling against one another. One half told her to run towards the boy. To know he was okay. To help him. To feel the immediate comfort and security of his arms. But the other half begged her to resist if she ever wanted to see him again.

When Ben finally came to, letting out a soft moan and rolling slightly to his side, Sarah released a sigh that unburdened the crushing weight of her worst fear.

Suddenly, something heavy blasted down into the pit, sending colored orbs flying in every direction like a bomb had gone off. But it wasn't a bomb—that would be quick and painless. This was much worse. This destroyer had come in the form of a thrashing beast, and it had landed only a few feet from her.

Sarah could tell from the way everything moved around her that it was circling the pit—or circling *her*. Alfie waded through the sea of plastic balls, appearing to savor the sensation as his outstretched hands dragged by his sides. Every time he would reach a corner, he'd turn automatically as if programmed to do so. The seemingly endless act was agonizing for Sarah. She bit down on her bottom lip so hard that she tasted the unmistakable flavor of blood.

As he approached another corner, Alfie sharply changed course. He headed straight to the middle of the pit, sloshing aside armfuls of brightly colored playthings until he reached his destination.

As the soft, clacking noises began to subside and the plastic balls settled, so too did Alfie. Sarah seized the final opportunity to fill her lungs with air and held her breath. She had to. Even though she couldn't see him, Sarah could tell he was very close now, and she couldn't risk being heard or disturbing the easily manipulated surface that concealed her. Besides, she was a swimmer. Sarah had been inadvertently training for this moment her whole life.

She closed her eyes to steady her emotions. When they opened, she found herself looking straight up at Alfie towering directly above her.

Sarah thought he was looking right at her, but it was difficult to tell. She could only see his face in splintered pieces, made up from the slivers between the kaleidoscope of colored balls.

All at once Alfie's body went completely rigid. Sarah remembered seeing the same behavior when he was underneath the air duct. Once again, his head slowly slumped back, and his oval eyes began their unsettling routine of lazily opening and closing one by one. Then, abruptly, both eyes shot open, and Alfie's head locked back into a forward-facing position.

Sarah still wasn't positive that Alfie knew she was there, but it was hard to believe that he didn't. If she jumped up and made a run for it, he would slay her before she could get two steps away. Sarah couldn't believe the situation she had found herself in. She couldn't even breathe. The only thing left was to hope and pray.

Looking up at Alfie was like torture. He was going to do what he was going to do, and there was nothing Sarah could do about it. So instead she focused her sights on Ben. A single tear slid softly down her cheek. She didn't want to see what was coming—she just wanted to lose herself in him.

Sarah had not moved a muscle or taken a breath in what seemed like forever. She was denying her body its most autonomous function, and it was damning her for doing so. She suddenly became very aware of her heartbeat as it pounded its cadence from her chest straight up to her head. Her stomach began to convulse as her starving lungs begged for oxygen. She felt a tingling sensation in her moist palms as her brain began to drift. Despite all this she continued to hold. She would rather drown by suffocation than the alternate death possibly staring her in the face.

Alfie looked down at his left hand, wide open with claws splayed, then to his right hand gripping the knife. He lifted his head then turned around and began to walk away. Sarah had done it. She had outlasted her hunter.

Once he was out of sight, she carefully exhaled the used air, fighting the urge to take it all back in at once. The unbearable tension immediately melted into a stable calm. Now she just had to get Ben.

Without warning Alfie spun around wielding the knife high above his head. His arm plunged through the air and he stabbed Sarah deep in her stomach. She burst out of the ball pit, emitting a scream so raw and piercing that it threatened to annihilate her vocal cords.

The sound of Sarah's scream instantly snapped Ben's eyes open. He slid out of his semi-unconscious state and looked towards the ball pit to see Alfie standing triumphantly over the only thing that really mattered. "Sarah!" he shouted.

Ben pulled himself up and dove towards the severed ax head that was still lying right where it had broken off during his last encounter with Meaty. With the cold, steel block in hand, he sprinted towards the forked roads of fate.

As Ben neared the ball pit, the scene before him was

almost too much to grasp. It was all happening so fast. There was no time for a plan, no time for anything. He wrapped his fingers through the small squares of the net, tugging furiously at it. "Get away from her you bastard!" he yelled. Alfie looked over his shoulder at Ben, his devilish eyes squinting just enough to suggest there was a smile hidden below. As Ben looked on helplessly, the beast swung his head back towards Sarah. In a single, frantic downward thrust he stabbed into her body one more time. "Saaaaraaaah!!" Ben screamed.

Alfie walked slowly and calmly towards the netted wall on the opposite side of the ball pit from Ben. Although there was the small opening on that side, Alfie could not be bothered to take one step out of his way or to duck through it. Instead, with one swipe of his claws, he tore a hole into the netting right in front of him and stepped through.

Ben began desperately cutting through the net with the ax head. There were now two openings on the other side, but it would have taken almost as long to run over to them. More importantly, Alfie was on that side, and he couldn't risk getting into an altercation with him right now. After one long cut had been made, Ben started ripping through the netting with his bare hands. On the opposite side of the ball pit he saw Alfie walk away into the shadows.

Sarah was lying on her back, still buoyantly afloat atop the plastic ocean. Her hands clasped tightly to the wounds on her stomach as her breathing came in short bursts. She couldn't escape the faint red light from above, gently attempting to lure her to sleep. A comforting fog began to roll into the recesses of her conscious. But she fought to stay awake because she knew that Ben was coming. She would get to see him again. No matter what happened, in that moment, it meant that everything would be okay.

Ben had managed to tear a hole in the netting big enough to squeeze through and jumped into the pit. He waded over to Sarah as fast as he could, feeling the drag of a thousand unified spheres. As he got close he treaded lightly, being careful not to jostle her about where she lay.

Sarah could feel Ben near. She wanted to look into his eyes once more and hold onto his hand. She wanted to feel the warmth and tenderness radiate from his body. She didn't have to hear the words to know that he felt the same way. Looking up at the red light, he entered her vision, and she got to see him again.

Ben slid a hand gently behind Sarah's head, lifting her up and cradling her in his arms. As he surveyed her wounds, tears flooded his eyes. He blinked them away and swallowed hard at the lump in his throat—he didn't want her to be afraid.

"Sarah," he said, wrapping his hand around hers.

It took all her strength to reach up and rest her fingers on his cheek. "Hey," she said.

"You're gonna be alright," Ben said, wholeheartedly believing his own words. "I just need to get you out of here."

He tried to lift her as delicately as possible, but Sarah winced in pain. "No," she said, her trembling voice conveying the same thing her expression did. Ben wouldn't give into it, but the truth of the situation shot through his heart like a spear, and he laid her back down.

"Please don't go. Don't leave me," he said, unable to stop the tears that were now falling freely from his eyes.

Sarah looked past Ben at the tube maze behind them.

"Remember the last time we were here?" she asked with the faintest hint of a grin.

"I told you, that was some other kid," Ben said, sniffling through a soft laugh.

Sarah laughed too, but it sent a shudder through her weakened body. Ben flinched and pulled back slightly, having no idea what to do. He just held her hand tighter.

"I love you Ben," she said, and it was truly the most beautiful thing he had ever heard.

"You have no idea," Ben said. "I've loved you my entire life."

Sarah's pain dulled and was replaced by a euphoric sureness that she had never felt before. The love-warmth spread throughout her entire being, and she felt nothing but happiness. She smiled at Ben and nodded—they had both gone through the same journey to arrive where they were now.

She looked at him wistfully. "Maybe I'll wake up and we'll still be in the photo booth together," she said.

"Yeah, we just fell asleep," Ben replied, gently pulling her closer.

Ben could tell there wasn't much time left. If he could stop it at that very moment, he would be content to drift off into eternity with her right then and there.

"I'm so tired," Sarah said, her eyelids slowly opening and closing. "I think I'll wake up now."

"Wake up angel," Ben said, softly stroking her hair.

He looked down at her and saw his world in her eyes. She looked up at him and felt his soul. She could no longer lift her arm so instead she grabbed onto his. "I'll see you later," Sarah said, and when she closed her eyes this time, they didn't reopen.

A soft breath escaped her lips, and the gentle rise and fall of her chest ceased.

Ben's head dropped down as if the life had been drawn out of him too. He rested his forehead against hers and sobbed freely. His body heaved as the all-consuming grief smothered him, and the love he felt became indistinguishable from the pain. It was as though his entire reason for being had just been extinguished. As if a piece of his very soul had been taken from him and sent along with her. Maybe it had.

As his tears began to subside, Ben gained enough composure to focus on what he had to do next. He placed a tender kiss on Sarah's forehead and released her from his arms. She didn't sink down into the pit, but instead floated atop the brightly colored sea.

Before walking away, Ben took one more long look at her. "I'll see you soon," he said.

CHAPTER TWENTY-ONE

If from the greatest love Ben's heart could imagine was born the worst pain he could fathom, the two combined to conjure the most blinding fury he had ever felt. As if the lights above were a physical manifestation of his hate, Ben was seeing red. Searing, scalding, scorch-the-earth red. And it was all singularly focused on only one thing—the wolf.

Ben stomped through the rows of games, looking back and forth aggressively. "Where are you?!" he screamed at the top of his lungs. "I said where are you?!!"

He didn't have a weapon or a plan, and he didn't care. He just wanted Alfie in front of him.

A slight movement from behind spun him around. "Come on you chicken shit! I'm still standing!"

Ben had gone berserk, willing to take on the devil himself if he appeared. But he'd have to settle for the next closest thing. His nerve endings buzzed with an electric rage that he felt pooling in his white-knuckled fists. Hot, ragged breath shot in and out of his flared nostrils. This time he was the wild animal.

He anticipated. He waited impatiently. But nothing emerged from around a shady corner. Nobody jumped in his path. He was tired of being hunted. He was tired of playing games. He just wanted vengeance.

"You coward! You COWARD! Hide then! I'll find you!" Ben shouted.

In the silent room those last three words began repeating back to him ominously, over and over, in the form of a whisper. "I'll find you. I'll find you. I'll find you…" Ben quickly turned this way and that, but it was like the source was always right behind him. Then it started coming from everywhere—a thousand voices overlapping into a maddening crescendo, surrounding him as they dug into his brain. The hairs stood up on the back of his neck, tugging his skin into tiny, shivery goose bumps. But the anger he felt overwhelmed any momentary fear. He wouldn't let this place get to him anymore. There was nothing else they could take from him.

Then the whispers abruptly stopped.

Ben took a hurried glance around the room, expecting to see Alfie at any second. But he was nowhere to be found. Then something cut through his hatred, threatening to disarm his razor edge. It was *her*. Thoughts of Sarah tugged at the corners of his beleaguered mind, but he kept them at bay, knowing they would disable him if he let them. He needed to stay clear-headed and ready for the enemy that would eventually come.

Alfie.

Alfie.

Alfie.

As if Ben had willed him into sight, the wolf stepped out from behind an arcade at the other end of the room. Ben glared with a teeth-baring snarl that rivaled that of his opponent. Alfie glared back, but Ben didn't waver—his eyes stayed fixed on the

193

monster's. He was determined to make sure Alfie knew he wasn't afraid and that he wouldn't back down.

Alfie was still gripping the knife that had taken Ben's everything. He lifted it proudly, turning the blood-soaked blade over as he admired the memento of his work. He wiped it across his fur as Ben watched and seethed. Alfie began swaying his head back and forth, huffing and grunting as he gnashed his fangs over and over.

With his head still thrashing madly about, the beast started to advance. Ben took a few steps back in response to the unnerving sight, but he didn't cower. He kept his shoulders squared and his jaw clenched. This is what he wanted. This is what he sought out.

Ben's hand brushed up against the side of his jeans as he moved. He was confused at first—then it hit him, and he couldn't believe what he'd forgotten about in his pocket this whole time. His hand discretely slipped into the rigid denim lining as he tried to mask his reaction to the fortunate discovery. He pulled out Brad's pocket knife and unfolded it inconspicuously by his side.

While Ben was stealthily unsheathing his newly found weapon, he had unintentionally backed himself up against a wall. As soon as he made contact with it, Alfie charged.

It all happened in a blur. There was no time to think, only react. Ben's whole body tensed, and he unleashed a roar so loud and full of anguish that it made even Alfie flinch. Ben raised the knife overhead. And they clashed. Ben plunged his knife into Alfie's eye just as the monster's blade tore through his side.

Alfie recoiled, stumbling backwards with the pocket knife embedded so deeply in his eye socket that only the hilt was exposed. Ben was hunched over. With his adrenaline racing he was more in shock than in pain as he clenched his wound. Alfie recovered quickly and lunged towards Ben like some sort of cycloptic nightmare-demon with dark green liquid oozing from his ruptured eye.

Alfie grabbed Ben by the throat. His jointy fingers were so long that they almost touched each other as they wrapped around the back of Ben's neck. With his sharp claws digging into Ben's skin, Alfie pinned him up against the wall.

Ever so slowly Alfie lifted Ben. He moved him up until the tips of his shoes scraped frantically against the ground. Alfie held him at that height, relishing in Ben's distress as he looked down at his captive's shuffling feet. Alfie continued to lift him until he was several feet off the ground. Ben felt as though the overextended tendons in his neck would snap at any second.

Ben tried to kick at the wolf, but with his wound he couldn't even manage to lift his legs, let alone kick with any power. Alfie held him dangling there, and in that position the boy was helpless.

The laceration on Ben's side was steadily losing blood. Combined with the partial asphyxiation from Alfie's choke hold, it caused a wave of dizziness to wash over him.

Alfie held out the long knife and splayed out his hand until it slid between his fingers and fell to the floor. He reached up to the handle protruding from his eye and withdrew the pocket knife as thick, green liquid spurted and gurgled out from the gash. He rested the blade against Ben's face and tapped it under his quivering eye three times. It was a sadistic retaliation, and Ben had accepted this was how he was going to die. Alfie drew back the blade along with his head. His functioning eye rolled back while the other one, filled with pussing discharge, was stuck twitching rapidly in place.

Ben mustered his remaining strength for a last-ditch offensive. Pinned and hanging against the wall though, he was without a weapon and could barely lift his legs. His arms, fully extended, couldn't even reach Alfie's head or chest, so he was resigned to pounding his fists futilely against the metal arm of his attacker.

Ben began to get so weak from the lack of oxygen that the pounding became tapping, and soon he was simply going through the motions. The only thing he had control over as Alfie held the blade high above him was whether to open or close his eyes. And so he waited, eyes wide open, not giving an inch of pride to the bastard before him. Alfie's grip tightened around Ben's neck, and the room started to spin as he braced for the end.

All of a sudden a monstrous arm with long, brown fur and curled, black claws emerged above Alfie's head. Ben was stunned as he tried to process what he was seeing.

What the hell was that?!

Ben squeezed his eyes shut and shook his head. When he opened them, the long claws of the oversized paw were clasped under Alfie's chin. In a flash of vicious savagery the paw ripped the wolf's head damn near completely off his body. It was left dangling by his side, attached by only a thin flap of skin. And yet somehow, he continued to stand... continued to move.

The grip on Ben's neck immediately loosened, and he dropped from where he had been suspended in mid-air. He was so depleted that his legs buckled, and he collapsed to the ground. As he gasped for breath, Ben was baffled by the possibility of there being yet another robotic predator in the building. That just couldn't be. But he knew what he *thought* he saw.

Ben waited for his eyes to refocus then looked up. Alfie's body was convulsing but still upright for now. And what Ben saw standing behind the headless corpse finally gave him his answer. There he was, fully revealed with a brand new, damned grizzly bear arm. It was Meaty.

Ben was instantly jarred back to life, the hazy feeling of transient weakness passing like a dizzy spell after a bad cut on a finger. He watched as Alfie began to slump down, like the air being let out of a balloon. Before he could fall though, Meaty held out an arm, and Alfie folded over it like a jacket draped on a chair back.

The whole scene was bat-shit crazy, and Ben had not even had a second to comprehend what the hell was going on. A bewildering cocktail of relief, panic and awe raced through his bloodstream. He had felt so faint that he must have missed Meaty walking up behind his soon-to-be victim. But the towering goliath stood there now, clenching the carcass of his former ally with his originally endowed arm. On the opposite side of his torso, Meaty rolled the new limb around in its socket a few times, feeling satisfied with the symbiosis after its first test.

Meaty leaned in until he and Ben were face to face. Mere inches away, he slowly opened his mouth, and it smelt like the bowels of a mechanic's garage on a sweltering day. Ben could tell the creature was straining to do something, but he didn't know what. Somehow, through evolution, the supernatural or plain sheer will, Meaty managed to force out several unintelligible sounds. His mouth was open the whole time, though he attempted to imitate speaking by moving his jaw slightly up and down. With a dreadfully deep voice, Meaty painstakingly forged his first two words— "Youurrrᴢe... miiiine."

Alfie hung limp and unmoving over Meaty's arm, except for his mouth which was still snapping open and shut. Suddenly, his body jolted back to life. With his head still hanging grotesquely at his side, Alfie's limbs flailed wildly about, trying to maim anything they could touch. He wielded the pocket knife chaotically through the air as it stabbed into Meaty's abdomen over and over again. The blade wasn't inflicting any real damage though, only managing to further enrage the monster.

One of Alfie's hands blindly brushed against Meaty's open mouth and instantly grabbed ahold. Razor-sharp claws sunk deep inside, and as hard as his arm was pulling down, it could have easily ripped the lower face off a human. Stressed pistons within Meaty's jaw whined as he chomped down with the unrelenting force of a hydraulic press. Four long, black fingers hung out of Meaty's mouth, like a giant tarantula trying to escape. Meaty spit the fingers onto the floor then lifted Alfie up until they were eye to eye.

Ben seized the opportunity and slid out of the way, taking off running towards a cluster of arcades that offered cover. From there he watched the carnage ensue.

Still draped over an arm, Alfie was a little too close for the savagery Meaty had in store for him. He grabbed Alfie by the wrist and held the defenseless beast out like bait on a hook. Black fur flew in the air as Meaty's freshly acquired limb butchered Alfie, tearing across and into his shuddering body. Ben could tell it wasn't a real limb though—it was another animatronic appendage. At least the mechanics were. For all he knew the fur was real and so were the half-foot claws.

But Ben had never seen this one before. Whether the arm had come from a long-forgotten creature or one yet-to-be created was irrelevant. All Ben knew was that Meaty had now evolved into some sort of super-hybrid, even stronger and more lethal than he had been before.

Alfie was still dangling in the air, but Meaty was almost done with him seeing as how there wasn't a whole lot more left to maul. Even after the beating he'd just endured, Alfie's head was still connected by the thin flap of skin. It was almost as if Meaty *wanted* it to stay on.

He lifted Alfie high and drew back the grizzly bear arm as far as he could. It shot forward like a screaming hell-canon and didn't stop until it burst through the other side of Alfie's chest.

Ben savored every ounce of brutality inflicted onto the wolf, but he never lost sight of the cold truth that the enemy of his enemy… was still his enemy.

Ben ducked back behind the arcade he was peeking out from. He leaned his head back against the machine, troubled by the one question he couldn't answer. *Why didn't Meaty kill me when he had the chance?*

Ben knew he couldn't let himself think too much into it. Someway, somehow, he was still alive, although not for much longer if he didn't tend to the bloodletting wound in his side. He needed to find a place to buy some time. He scanned the building as far as he could see, desperately searching for inspiration. As his eyes passed the stage area, they stopped.

Bingo.

Ben glanced back at Meaty who was still entangled with Alfie, and he decided to make a run for it.

Although Alfie's life force was nearing its end, he was still clawing, stabbing and biting at any part of Meaty he could get ahold of. Meaty grabbed the wolf's shoulders and slammed him into the wall, forcing the knife that was unbelievably still in his hand to drop. But the limbs continued to jerk, as if a low voltage electrical current ran through them. Meaty surged forward and smashed Alfie completely through the wall, this time with such devastating might that the building trembled. He snatched him out of the giant hole, and Alfie's outbursts came to a halt.

Meaty lifted the carcass up for a final inspection. Everything was dead except for Alfie's one good eye, still glaring and twitching in defiance. Meaty placed Alfie's head between his hands and squeezed so hard that the metal skull began to crack. Dark green liquid seeped out of Alfie's eye sockets like Meaty was juicing an orange. He tilted the head to face him and shook it violently before realizing that finally, the wolf was dead.

Meaty dropped the lifeless body, and it slumped down into a heap on the floor. He nudged the pile of limbs with his foot and waited, then turned around from the remains of his now-expired bandmate.

And then there were two.

CHAPTER TWENTY-TWO

Ben had made it to the broom closet right beside the stage. He knew the hanging bulb probably wouldn't work since the rest of the building was without power, but he couldn't help give it a shot anyway. As expected, it didn't turn on. Ben was forced to leave the door cracked open so that just enough red light could ease through for him to see.

He would have to be quiet. Really quiet. If Meaty walked up on him in that tiny room then that was it. There was no place to hide and certainly nowhere to run. But Ben had accepted that risk and for good reason. He knew the supplies in that closet by heart, and he knew it contained two sure things that could help him. He had also thought ahead for when Meaty would inevitably make his way over to that side of the building. He just wasn't sure if it would work.

Ben looked up, and laying on top of a shelf was a bag of clean work rags, exactly where he expected them to be. He pushed aside some odds and ends, then reached into a frayed shoebox labeled "misc." and dug out a half-used roll of duct tape. Before he got to work though, he had to make sure that one last thing was there.

The only toolbox in Marinara was big and red, and it had a name. "Big Red" was scrawled across its lid with the penmanship of a three-year-old. It was not referred to as a toolbox but rather by its given name by anyone who was anyone.

Everybody eventually encountered Big Red because it was huge and contained an absolute ton of random stuff. Hammers, staples, drill bits, glue, WD-40—whatever one needed, short of a raise, was all in there. For that reason, and also because Marinara was in a constant state of decay, it was used constantly and left all over the building. It wasn't uncommon for the upper echelon of power to be yelling and cussing over who the hell had the toolbox last. And Ben was not exempt of guilt. Matter of fact he was one of the worst culprits.

Once he was asked to screw in a drooping vent outside the building. Ben figured he would extend the project by hiding a cheeseburger with extra mayo and all the fixins inside the toolbox and have an outdoor picnic. Legend had it that quality control manager Darcy came running out screaming that a kid had gotten so nervous while pulling up a toy that he'd puked all over the claw machine. Half of her excitement was for Ben to help clean it off the control panel pronto. The other half was pure teenage bliss that it had actually happened and that Ben needed to see the drenching to fully appreciate it.

Darcy rambled on. The whole affair did sound lovely. And while the puke was a nice added bonus, it wasn't nearly as monumental as the first toy possibly being pried from the claw's iron grip. Ben Cooper always did, and always would, despise that notoriously stingy black hole of tokens.

"But did he get the toy?!" he interjected.

"Yes," Darcy responded, then pointed at his cheeseburger. "And that's a write-up."

Needless to say, the toolbox was forgotten in the beating sun for several days before anyone found it, and Ben had to pick out the slimy, molded burger chunks before hosing the whole thing down.

And there it was—its fire engine red paint peeking out from under a shelf. Another fond memory or two popped into Ben's head then left just as soon as they had arrived. He gently picked up the toolbox and set it down next to the door.

Ben ripped off four long strips of duct tape and lightly hung them from the sink behind him. He reached for the bag of clean work rags on top of the shelf, wincing slightly and holding his side as he did. He pulled out one of the clean white rags and folded it over on itself until it was a quarter of its original size. Ben looked at the handwritten sign that read: "Your mother doesn't work here, put things back where you got them!" as he tossed the remaining bag of rags in the sink behind him. He pressed the square cloth against his wound and began to pick off the strips of duct tape to hold it in place. It wasn't perfect but it would do—at least for what he had to get done.

Ben slid an eye into the crack of the door and was startled to see Meaty right there in the dining pit looking around. Ben was sure he would have heard the rumbling behemoth approaching, but he seemed to be moving discreetly now on purpose. Whereas earlier Meaty had been launching tables in the air, he was now sidestepping them and carefully looking both under and around them without making a noise.

Ben had known that this time would come, and he was betting everything that he had a way to get past the monster. He just didn't have a plan for afterward. How could he take on Meaty? There were no more axes, no more electrical traps and certainly no bigger monsters to come along and unexpectedly save him from the baddest one of them all.

Ben racked his brain for ideas but nothing came, and the ones that did didn't make sense. Then he saw it. A little rusted can labeled "machine grease." It was like a firework went off in his brain, each mini explosion connecting together one by one to form the sequence of his master plan. *Holy shit, that might just work*, he thought.

Ben would have to gather multiple items throughout Marinara though. If he failed to obtain even one of them the whole plan would fall apart. He needed some time, and he needed Meaty distracted—that's where Big Red came in.

Ben flipped the latch and opened the lid. He whispered something inaudible to the inanimate object then peeked out the door. There was no Meaty in sight. With the toolbox in hand, Ben opened the door and covertly walked the four to five paces to the top of the basement stairs.

With one last wide-eyed glance over his shoulder, Ben hurled the toolbox down the pitch-black staircase. He purposefully aimed for the bottom of the stairs to make first impact as opposed to letting the box fling objects all the way down. He wanted Meaty to walk down the entire staircase before even having a clue as to what was going on.

In the deafening silence of the building, the toolbox crashed with about as much clamor as a bulldozer. The fortuitous throw also blasted the basement door open, which would gift Ben an even longer window of opportunity if Meaty decided to investigate the room.

Ben wasted no time in dashing back to the broom closet, completely shutting the door behind him. There he stood in the dark—waiting, listening.

Almost immediately Ben heard footsteps barreling towards the noise. His heart raced as Meaty approached. He knew what would happen if the closet door suddenly opened right in front of him.

The footsteps stopped. Ben listened hard for a clue, but he had no idea what was happening on the other side of the door. *Just walk down. Just walk down. Just walk down,* Ben found himself silently chanting.

The sound of weighty footsteps began going down the staircase, and as they faded, so did the thumping of Ben's heart.

It was go time.

He crept out of the closet and, for a fleeting second, looked down at the staircase, wondering if there was any way he could trap Meaty down there. The basement door did have a lock, but he'd have to find the spare keys. Then Ben snapped out of it. *How damn stupid,* he thought. He couldn't believe he'd actually considered following Meaty down there and risking his life to lock a flimsy basement door on him. It would be as futile as using a paper shield to protect from a sword. Ben got his focus back on the task at hand and started running towards the gaming floor.

As he ran, looking for the first thing he needed, a surreal feeling came over Ben. He realized there were no more threats other than the one he had just left in the basement. Nothing would be hiding around the next corner, neither friend nor foe.

It was a gut-wrenching reminder that he was the only one left. Just him and a seven-foot robotic Sasquatch with a grizzly bear arm, trapped in a haunted building with nowhere to go but right at each other.

Ben crouched down behind the air hockey table to catch his breath. He knew the first item was around there somewhere; at least that was where he'd seen it last. Then he spotted it—a blunt reminder of the happy dream he was having before diving into this inescapable nightmare. The Janitor's giant, almost two-liter bottle of Jack Daniels was perched atop an arcade machine where it had been left in another life.

Ben grabbed it and noticed the bit of empty space at the top where Brad had taken a swig from it. He was instantly whisked back to the air hockey game with all of his friends and the great time they'd shared. Keaton had been scoring goals at will and making sure everyone was drunk and happy. He always did shine in moments like that. A little voice spoke in Ben's head.

Do it for Keaton.

Ben gripped the bottle tighter, staring at the contents that would never be drank. How fast things could all change. They had *just* been there, *always* been there, and now they were gone.

Ben pulled up the side of his shirt. The white rag he had fashioned into a bandage was now soaked red. He pulled his shirt back down, paying it no more mind. He had to finish, for them, and for everyone who had come before them. Maybe this was his fate—he just had to meet it in the middle.

Ben looked towards the basement staircase. He could hear a steady rustling echoing up the concrete passage and knew that Meaty was searching the room. *Well done, Big Red*, he thought to himself. The coast was clear, at least for now.

Ben brazenly stepped out into the open. Still alert, still wary, but with the determined gait of a man on a mission. The whiskey bottle was tilted upside down, pouring out a trail of alcohol as he strolled towards his next destination.

As he approached the demolished prize counter, Ben's eyebrows scrunched down. *What the hell happened here?*

He looked down at the broken glass, and then he remembered. It was *him* that Meaty had thrown into the damn thing. Maybe it was the lingering effects of a concussion or the fact that he had been thrown into or smashed up against about everything in the building and was losing track. Either way, it was that kinda night.

Ben set down the empty bottle of Jack and looked at all the plastic rings, sunglasses and bracelets mixed amongst the shattered wood and glass. He knelt down and started brushing aside debris. By sheer luck he found what he needed under the first pile. He shoved it into his back pocket and got to his feet. As he walked out of the wreckage Ben saw a box of dented Runts in front of him. He paused for a few, long seconds, then stepped over them. He grabbed the empty bottle and continued along his way.

Do it for Sarah.

Ben came up to the kitchen entrance and stalled. He needed something in there, but he also knew what he would see when he opened that flapping door. Ben took a deep breath and steadied his mind. He glanced through the plastic window, almost half-expecting to see Perry poke his head up with a chef's hat on. That was how he would remember his friend.

Once inside, Ben kept his eyes down, resisting the unnaturally natural urge to look at his friends' bodies. The floor was covered in red. Ben headed straight towards the fryer, being careful not to slip in the sauce as he walked. Along the way he saw one of Chrissy's legs in his peripheral vision and cursed the beings that put her there.

He tilted the neck of the whiskey bottle down into the grease, making sure not to lose his grip as he did so. When it was filled all the way to the brim, he screwed the cap back on and wiped off the excess. With his task completed Ben headed for the exit. He softly kicked open the flapping door and walked out, his head filled with images of the friends he just left behind.

Do it for Perry.

Do it for Chrissy.

Ben was shaken as he came out of the kitchen. It was a grueling undertaking to have endured, and he knew the next one wouldn't be any easier. Not because of what he needed but where it was located. As he approached the front door to Marinara, Ben became numb. Almost as if his mind and body were shocking him out of feeling anything, knowing he couldn't take much more. He knew rationally he had to resist his mind flooding with emotion. He needed to remain clear, composed and calculated. The task simply had to get done, and there was no way around it.

But as he approached the front door and the letter jacket came into view, Ben lost it. There was no way to avoid seeing his friend or the devastating state he was left in. Ben tried to fight back the tears, but they fell of their own accord. He crouched down and reached gently into Brad's jacket pocket, pulling out the lighter he always kept there.

Do it for Brad.

Ben touched his friend on the shoulder, looking away before the streams threatened to break the dam. "Thanks buddy."

He now had everything he would need.

CHAPTER TWENTY-THREE

The faintest strains of music wafted down into the underbelly of Marinara where Meaty prowled within the inky, permeating shadows. The tune was indistinct but familiar, and the beast's ear twitched as he turned towards the sound. He had been in the basement for a while, sure that Ben had made his way there before him. He had searched the room high and low, dissecting every inch but paying no mind to the two corpses in the middle of it, for death was no longer a curiosity to him.

As it dawned on Meaty that his search had been futile, he walked over to the basement door and ripped it off its hinges. He took his time going up the steps, marring inch deep claw marks into one side of the wall as he passed.

Meaty emerged from the staircase, and the tune became louder and clearer—it was a song by his own band, The Toppings. His head turned left and then right, sweeping the room for any signs of the music's origin. Like a bloodhound picking up a scent, Meaty's ear locked onto the direction of the sound and he began to track it.

The music seemed to be getting louder the closer he got to the dining pit. As he stood in the middle of the pit he looked up at the stage. It was clearly coming from somewhere in that area. The acoustics of the hollow platform intensified and projected the volume of the music, as if it were being played by an invisible, ghostly ensemble. Meaty vaulted onto the stage and headed right towards the center of it. Though still muffled, the music was the loudest it had been now, and he looked down at the trapdoor beneath his feet. Meaty dropped to one knee and with a single, thunderous punch shattered the door into pieces.

The darkness and the dust obscured his view initially as he peered down into the hole. As the swirling particles dissipated the source was finally revealed—a plastic, wind-up "radio" sitting on the first step. Meaty picked the prize counter toy up and curiously inspected the small, peculiar item. A picture of his face adorned a colorful sticker on the radio's front, while one of the band's patented showtunes played at a surprisingly loud volume from its speaker.

Ben could hear the music from where he was hiding next to the square slide above. Meaty had taken the bait and was right where he wanted him on the stage below. It was now or never. Ben sat with his knees tucked against his chest and leaned his forehead onto his folded arms. He closed his eyes. He wasn't going to wait for his life to flash before them. Rather, he made the conscious choice to recall all the people closest to him.

Images of loved ones rolled one into the other across the blank canvas of his mind. His immediate family. His best friends. *Her.* And even a few others who unexpectedly popped into his head—his favorite teacher, his old bus driver, his neighbor's barking dogs who would quiet down as soon as he reached over the fence and gave them some attention. Ben's

211

heart was full as he felt the comforting reassurance of a well-lived and well-loved, albeit short, life. He said a silent prayer then opened the lighter and struck up a flame.

Meaty was standing in the middle of the stage now, slowly rotating the still-playing radio in his hands with waning interest. A glint of fire in the dark room caught his peripheral vision, and he turned his head towards the light.

Ben was standing in the center of the hollow square high atop the dining pit. His appearance was rough. He looked beaten and worn. His face was bruised, his hair disheveled. One sleeve had been ripped off his now blood-soaked t-shirt which stuck like syrup to his side.

In Ben's hand was the giant bottle of Jack. Dull, brown grease dripped down the side of the bottle and trickled over his fingers. The missing sleeve of his t-shirt was hanging down its glass neck, and at the end of the cloth burned a long flame, flickering and dancing against the darkness. It was a massive Molotov Cocktail.

Ben stood tall, the warmth of the flame licking his forearm as he gripped the ignited bomb. The sight was nothing short of epic, taken straight out of the apex of an ancient heroic poem. The lone survivor, battered yet doggedly perseverant as he basked in the fortunate advantage of having both the high ground and the element of surprise.

Meaty leaned over and carefully set the radio down, then straightened back up. It was winding down now, emitting a slowed, distorted version of a Toppings song.

The two stood, boldly defiant of one another.

Right as the monster took his first step forward, Ben hurled the bottle through the air.

He knew it was a dead on shot the second he let it go. Nevertheless, Ben held his breath and time seemed to slow down as he watched it arch over the dining pit. As soon as the bottle made impact with Meaty's metal chest, it exploded with a glass-shattering shriek and he erupted instantaneously into an enormous fireball.

Vicious flames covered every inch of his body, rippling across his fur in a beautifully hypnotic dance. Meaty staggered slightly back, looking down at his limbs in a mild state of confusion. He steadied himself, then raised his head and looked directly towards Ben.

Meaty launched off the stage, landing with a ground shaking thud into the dining pit. He barreled through the piles of upturned tables, igniting a literal warpath of fire in his wake.

Ben's mouth fell open as he watched the scene unfold below him. He'd expected Meaty to put up a fight, but he had not expected him to be unfazed. As the towering inferno continued to advance, Ben clutched his side and limped away as quickly as he could. He headed towards arcade row where, if needed, the final piece of his plan awaited.

Halfway down the row Ben collapsed. He was so tired. It would have been so easy to lay there and wait for death, but something wouldn't let him. Something inside demanded he keep going. If death was to come it was going to have to wait. Ben looked behind him and saw the crest of a fiery wave approaching the square slide from below.

Meaty walked up the slide, his weight and the blistering heat warping it beneath his feet with each step. As he reached the top, his shoulders were too broad to fit through the square opening, so he crashed straight through it, sending large pieces of melted, yellow plastic bursting off on all sides.

Get up! Ben silently yelled at himself. *GET UP!* His self-imposed command along with the sight of Meaty still marching towards him gave Ben just enough of an adrenaline jolt to get back to his feet. He stumbled down the aisle, one hand holding his side, the other leaving bloody smears as he propped himself up against every other arcade.

Ben reached the end of the row, this time giving his body permission to fall to the ground. The arcades were flush against the wall on that side, so there was only one way in and one way out. This was the end of the line.

With his back against the wall he blindly reached up, searching for what he knew was right above him. Just then Meaty turned the corner and arrived at the other end of the row. As Ben's fingers connected with the metal pull tab, he thought back to his heart-to-heart with Keaton earlier in the night.

He squeezed his fingers around the tab.

"Fuck it."

Ben yanked down on the fire alarm, knowing with reasonable certainty the dual outcomes that it would yield.

The sprinklers above burst to life, and a monsoon of cool rain fell over the entire building. Ben had been right in assuming the shoddy, untested system wouldn't come on automatically, which is why the plan was always to activate manually if needed. He just thanked God they actually worked.

As soon as the downpour of water hit the grease fire on Meaty, he detonated into a massive firestorm. The flames covering his body instantly doubled in size, shooting out at least five feet in every direction. The sound was immediate and intense, not unlike the distinct crackling of cold food hitting hot oil in a fryer.

The wild blaze made the beast look like a gatekeeper to the underworld. The heat was so extreme that Ben could feel it all the way from where he was sitting. Meaty had transformed into a walking supernova.

The tips of the flames reached the ceiling now, overwhelming the water and spreading quickly to the corners where they met the walls and travelled downwards. The whole building was soon engulfed.

Meaty trudged forward, hurling the arcades on either side of him as if they were flimsy cardboard boxes. His raw strength, even as he literally burned to death, was a sight to behold.

Finally, he began to weaken. Succumbing to the relentless destruction of the flames, Meaty sunk to a knee. Chunks of fur and skin had melted off his face, exposing the bare skeleton underneath. His enraged eyes, white teeth and crown were still there though, as a reminder of who he once was. The fire was so hot that the visible areas of his metal frame were glowing bright red. He just would not die.

Then Ben understood it. Meaty was fueled by hate. His will was not to live; it was to kill.

Meaty stood back up. He was halfway to his final victim, and there was nowhere else for Ben to run. He was severely injured, and he was trapped. But this was the endgame. It *had* to work.

Two more steps and Meaty fell again, this time to both knees. As he hit the ground his crown fell off his head. It rolled forward until it abruptly stopped—against the sole of Ben's shoe. Meaty lifted his hand towards the crown. The raindrops were hitting Ben's eyes, making him blink and squint, but he opened them wide as he glared at Meaty for what he was about to do next.

Ben kicked the crown forward, and it shot right past Meaty's side as he slowly swayed in place. With a severely delayed reaction, Meaty sluggishly turned his head to where the crown had just gone by and swiped hopelessly for it.

Overhead, the sprinklers had exhausted their supply and trickled to a stop. But the water had done its job, at least on Meaty. The flames were minimal on his body at this point, but it was clear he was dying.

Meaty turned his head back around and stared right at Ben. He wasn't able to express much with his melted, barren face, but Ben could tell that he was seething, and it brought him the slightest bit of satisfaction. The sound of screeching metal pierced Ben's ears as Meaty tried to stand again. But he couldn't. The intense heat had melted his joints. His legs were mangled under his weight, so he dragged himself forward with his arms. Several tubes on his body ruptured all at once, spraying brown liquid like a cut artery. Without warning, one of Meaty's arms gave way, and he slammed face-first into the ground. Ben pulled his legs back as Meaty was now only a few feet away.

As Meaty raised his head back up, Ben was aghast. He'd hit the ground hard. His metal skull had been heated to such extreme temperatures for so long that it had become malleable. Half of his smoldering face was completely caved in. Several of his boxy, white teeth lay on the floor beneath him, while the ones still in his mouth were left jagged and deranged. The fall had clearly broken his jaw as well, because it now swung wide open without any resistance. But none of this stopped him. Meaty kept coming.

He could only lift his head about a half foot off the ground as he edged forward. The bottom half of his mouth dragged behind his head like a plow, slowing him down as the shards of remaining teeth snagged and pulled up the carpet. Ben watched, entranced by the grotesquely disfigured monster in its final moments.

Suddenly a fiery hand lashed out, and Ben jolted back against the wall. Meaty's hand trembled in the air, just out of reach from its target. It was the grizzly bear arm. Ben could tell by the five charred claws right in front of his face.

The muscles in Ben's taut shoulders began to relax as he realized Meaty could advance no further. The fine line between death and triumph was but a few mere inches. And Ben was ready for his victory lap.

He looked past the trembling claws before him then down at Meaty one last time. "You're mine," Ben said, his words as quiet as a whisper but as intense as a stampede.

Meaty's hand reluctantly lowered to the ground, desperately reaching for the kill until the bitter end.

Ben cautiously waited as the body lay motionless, then he waited some more. It was still covered with small patches of burning flame, and Ben watched as it further disintegrated before his eyes.

It was over.

Ben combed his fingers into his hair and rested his forehead against his palm. The sudden flood of relief and accomplishment was so overwhelming that for a second he thought he might weep. But he held it together, exhaling a deep breath that he didn't realize he'd been holding in. His chest emptied, expelling any lingering anxiety that had been pent up inside. But in the process he noticed something strange—he could see his breath.

Ben looked around and flames were everywhere. While it should have felt scorching hot in there, Ben shivered and wrapped his arms tightly around himself. As he took in the menacing yet beautifully glowing room, he inhaled the sharp, chilled air and wondered if the building was doing this intentionally or not. It seemed so alive and yet as if it were dying at the same time.

Ben looked to his side and noticed a leftover bottle of whiskey sitting against the wall. By a stroke of luck it was just within reach. Even better it still had a few shots left inside. Ben leaned over as far as he could and coerced it towards himself with the tips of his fingers. He lifted it to his lips and took a swig, but he didn't swallow. He swished the bitter liquid around inside his mouth then spit it all over Meaty's carcass. One of the few, small patches of flames left burning on his back burst upward then quickly tapered back down. Ben leaned back and took a real drink, not completely enjoying the warm sensation as the bitter liquid washed down his throat, but more than he ever had before. All of a sudden the temperature was a bit more bearable.

Fire now hungrily consumed the paint and wood-paneled tinder of all the machines lining both sides of arcade row. The long, blazing path looked like a fantastical excerpt from Dante's Inferno come to life. Just then a large chunk of the ceiling collapsed and crashed to the ground a few feet away from where Ben was sitting. Farther down another piece broke off and landed on an arcade machine. It wouldn't be long now.

Ben reached into his pocket, grimacing as his body painfully reminded him of the gash in his side. Looking down he saw a small pool of blood gathered beside him. He pulled out the strip of photo booth pictures he had taken with Sarah. Those were just a few short hours ago, before this happy place turned into hell itself. *More like hell frozen over,* he thought as he huffed out a cloud of breath against the cold air. Ben smirked at his own joke. Sarah would've liked that one.

He held the strip of photos up close to get a good look at them. He noticed little details he hadn't before and felt the warm comfort of memory and love soak into his bones. His eyes slipped shut, and he brought the photos tightly against his chest. When his eyes opened, Ben tossed the empty whiskey bottle to the floor and rolled to his side. He attempted to stand but didn't have enough strength left. As he crawled away a trail of blood followed.

Ben made his way out of arcade row and turned his head towards the corner of his eye. He looked at the front door, which had somehow managed to avoid all flames so far. As the thought crossed Ben's mind, his eyes drifted for a brief moment. Then he swung his head back around and continued on. The building was crumbling all around him as Ben navigated through the blazing arcade room on hands and knees. Whenever he felt like giving up, he would look down at the strip of photos gripped in his hand and find the strength to keep going.

Just under the crackling of flames Ben could hear what sounded like moaning. It was all around him, as if it were coming from the building itself. The sound was like aged, broken-down vocal cords fused with slow, creaking wood. It wasn't quite human, but it was far more so than any noise an inanimate structure made of brick and lumber might produce. Whatever it was, it seemed like it was in pain. At least Ben hoped it was.

He reached the ball pit and gave everything he had to pull himself up the side. He looked like a boxer climbing the ropes in the twelfth round, determined to finish what he'd started. Ben slid through the cut in the netting then fell straight down into the delicate embrace of infinite plastic orbs. He made his way over to where Sarah's body rested and lay beside his love. Ben reached out for her hand and wove their fingers together. In his other hand he held tightly to the strip of photos.

Ben turned his head so that she was the only thing he could see. The crashing noise of the world falling apart around them faded to silence as he focused on her, and the surrounding flames cast a calm, golden glow over the two. He felt no fear now. Only love. He was completely at peace.

Ben's eyes drifted closed a few times, but he resisted the gentle tug as long as he could. He knew where he was going; he just wanted to stick around a little bit longer. A touch of red light entered his vision and he looked up. On the ceiling above, a hazy red emergency light was still on even after all that had happened. *At least something around here finally works,* he thought with a soft smile. The gentle tug became a gentle pull, and it was now too strong to resist. He held Sarah's hand tight. There was no more reason to resist. As Ben looked up, the red light turned to pure white…

…and they were together again.

CHAPTER TWENTY-FOUR

Bright, yellow sunlight eased through the glass-paned door to Marinara, extending a warm welcome throughout the entryway. The cheerful sound of children's laughter could be heard drifting up from the dining pit where a group of excited kids celebrated a birthday party, complete with paper hats and noisemakers that were driving their usually patient parents up the wall. The smell of pizza filled the air, and almost every arcade had a token-crazed boy or girl stationed in front of it, jabbing erratically at the controls.

Unnoticed amongst the commotion a lock quietly unclicked. The Janitor slipped out of his office, closing the door behind him. He looked over the crowd. The place was full of life today.

Just then, the speaker above the stage boomed a familiar voice, and the birthday party kids chanted along in unison: "Five, four, three, two, one... It's Showtime!"

Spotlights flickered and danced spontaneously across the red velvet curtains as the children screamed with joyful enthusiasm. "And now, Marinara proudly presents: the moguls of mozzarella, the sultans of sauce, the harbingers of heartburn..."

The curtains slowly drew back to reveal the highly anticipated act, and Meaty and The Toppings appeared in all their splendor.

The band came to life, bursting with one-liners and over-the-top, cheesy exuberance. Their mouths moved slightly off cue as they shifted about unnaturally, and the children adored them. Boys and girls united to cheer, sing-along and dance with wild abandon. And the beloved band played on.

****

No one noticed the small bird high above the dining pit, fluttering madly about and squinting its frightened eyes as it flew blindly into obstacles. It happened every now and then, and everyone had seen it before—a bird flying into a building in search of something, but inevitably discovering it can't get out.

In the midst of its panicked confusion, the bird spotted a familiar bright, yellow hue at the far end of the building. It quickly straightened its wings and headed for salvation. As it made an escape, through its bird's-eye view it saw Marinara revealed from above in all its bustling glory—from the frenzy of the stage area, through the game floor buzzing with a lively 8-bit soundtrack, past the prize counter offering countless mementos of an unforgettable day, to finally the sunlit entrance that would hopefully be its exit.

There was no slowing down from the path the bird was on. Either the door would open, or it wouldn't. A hand reached out for the handle and kindly held the door open for the rest of their party and then the next. The bird flew out over the parking lot and soared high into the safety of the sky where it could open its eyes at last.

On this beautiful Saturday afternoon, the parking lot was teeming with anxious crowds headed for food and fun. For every one adult walking towards Marinara there were two to three kids skipping beside them, so only half of the large lot was full. Most people had taken the coveted spots along the rows right in front of the building. But one vehicle stood apart. It sat strangely alone, parked towards the very far end of the lot away from all the others.

It was a blue Chevy short-bed pickup.

Printed in Great Britain
by Amazon

54436968R00128